CHOSEN
AS THE SHEIKH'S
ROYAL BRIDE

CHOSEN AS THE SHEIKH'S ROYAL BRIDE

JENNIE LUCAS

MILLS & BOON

First published in Great Britain 2019
by Mills & Boon, an imprint of HarperCollins*Publishers*
1 London Bridge Street, London, SE1 9GF

Large Print edition 2019

© 2019 Jennie Lucas

ISBN: 978-0-263-08261-6

MIX
Paper from
responsible sources
FSC® C007454

This book is produced from independently certified FSC™ paper to ensure responsible forest management. For more information visit www.harpercollins.co.uk/green.

Printed and bound in Great Britain
by CPI Group (UK) Ltd, Croydon, CR0 4YY

For Susan Mallery, Christine Rimmer,
and Teresa Southwick,

in gratitude for an amazing weekend
full of laughter, food, wine,
and brainstorming.

I couldn't have written this book
without you.

CHAPTER ONE

"You can't be serious!"

Omar bin Saab al-Maktoun, King of Samarqara, replied coldly to his vizier, "Always."

"But—a bride market?" The vizier's thin face looked shocked beneath the brilliant light from the throne room's high windows. "It hasn't been done in Samarqara in a hundred years!"

"Then it is past time," Omar replied grimly.

The other man shook his head. "I never thought you, of all people, would yearn for the old ways."

Rising abruptly from his throne, Omar went to the window and looked out at his gleaming city. He'd done much to modernize Samarqara since he'd inherited the kingdom fifteen years ago. Gleaming steel and glass skyscrapers now lined the edge of the sea, beside older buildings of brick and clay. "Not all my subjects are pleased by my changes."

"So you'd sell your private happiness to appease a few hardliners?" His adviser looked at him blankly. "Why not just marry the al-Abayyi girl, like everyone expects?"

"Half of my nobles expect it. The other half would revolt. They say Hassan al-Abayyi is powerful enough without his daughter becoming queen."

"They'd get over it. Laila al-Abayyi is your best choice. Beautiful. Dutiful." Ignoring Omar's glower, he added, "Marrying her could finally mend the tragedy between your families—"

"No," Omar said flatly. He'd spent his whole reign trying to forget what had happened fifteen years before. He wasn't going to marry Laila al-Abayyi and be forced to remember every day. Shoulders tight, he said, "Samarqara needs a queen. The kingdom needs an heir. A bride market is the most efficient way."

"Efficient? It's cold as hell. Don't do this," Khalid pleaded. "Wait and think it over."

"I'm thirty-six. I'm the last of my line. I've waited too long already."

"You'd truly be willing to marry a stranger?" he said incredulously. "When you know, by the laws of Samarqara, once she has your child, you can never divorce her?"

"I am well acquainted with our laws," Omar said tightly.

"Omar," his vizier said softly, using his first name by the rights of their childhood friendship, "if you marry a stranger, you could be sentencing yourself to a lifetime of misery. And for what?"

But Omar had no intention of sharing his feelings, even to his most trusted adviser. No man was willing to lay his deepest weakness bare. A king even less. "I've given my reasons."

Khalid narrowed his eyes. "What if all the kingdom united, and begged you to marry Laila al-Abayyi? Then you would do it?"

"Of course," Omar said, secure in the knowledge that it would never happen. Half of his nobles were Hassan al-Abayyi's minions, while the other half violently opposed the man and insisted Omar must choose a bride from a competing Samarqari family. "All that matters is my people."

"Yes," his vizier said, tilting his head thoughtfully. "So for them, you'd risk everything on an old barbaric tradition."

Omar's jaw tightened. "A thousand times and more, rather than risk Samarqara falling back into war."

"But—"

"Enough. I've made my decision. Find twenty

women who are brilliant and beautiful enough to be my queen. First make sure they are all willing to be my bride." Omar strode out of his throne room in a whirl of robes, calling back coldly, "And do it now."

Why had she been stupid enough to agree to this?

Beth Farraday looked right and left nervously inside the ballroom of the elegant Paris mansion—*hôtel particulier*, they'd called it, a private eighteenth-century palace with a private garden, worth a hundred million euros, in the seventh arrondissement, owned by Sheikh Omar bin Saab al-Maktoun, the King of Samarqara. Beth knew those details because she'd spent the last twenty minutes talking to the waitstaff. They were the people Beth felt most comfortable talking to here.

Gripping her crystal flute, she nervously gulped down a sip of expensive champagne.

She didn't belong with these glamorous women in cocktail dresses, all the would-be brides who'd been assembled here from around the world. Like a modern-day harem, she thought dimly, from which this unknown sheikh king would choose his queen.

The other nineteen women were so incredibly beautiful that they wouldn't have needed to lift a finger to get attention. Yet they'd all achieved amazing things. So far, Beth had met a Nobel Prize–winner, a Pulitzer Prize–winner, an Academy Award–winner. The youngest female senator ever to represent the state of California. A famous artist from Japan. A tech entrepreneur from Germany. A professional gymnast from Brazil.

And then there was Beth. The nobody.

She *so* didn't belong here, and she knew it.

She'd known it even before she'd taken the first-class commercial flight from Houston yesterday, and gotten on the private jet awaiting her in New York, where she'd met the other women traveling from North and South America. She'd known it from the moment her brainiac twin sister had asked her to take her place in this dog and pony show.

"Please, Beth," her sister had begged on the phone two days before. "You have to do it."

"Pretend to be you? Are you crazy?"

"I'd go myself, but I just barely saw the invitation." Beth wasn't surprised. She knew Edith had a habit of letting mail pile up, sometimes for weeks. "You know I can't leave my lab. I'm on the edge of a breakthrough!"

"You always think that!"

"You're much better at schmoozing anyway," her sister wheedled. "You know I'm no good with people. Not like you."

"And I'm totally princess material," Beth replied ironically, as she'd paused in pushing a broom around the thrift shop where she worked.

"All you have to do is show up at this event in Paris, and they'll give me a million dollars. Just think what this could mean to my research—"

"You always think you can make me do anything, just by telling me you're saving kids with cancer."

"Can't I?"

Beth paused.

"Yes," she'd sighed.

Which was why Beth was in Paris now. Wearing a red dress that was far too tight, because she was the only potential bride who didn't fit sample size. She didn't fit in, full stop. After being driven in a limo, like all the other women, from their luxury hotel on the avenue Montaigne to this over-the-top mansion, she'd spent the last few hours in this airless, hot ballroom, watching beautiful, accomplished women go up one by one to speak to a dark-eyed man in sheikh's robes, sitting in tyrannical splendor on the dais.

Except Beth. The sheikh's handlers seemed bewildered by what to do with her. They'd apparently already decided that she wasn't remotely their boss's type. With that, she fervently agreed.

She looked up at the scowling man sitting in his throne on the dais. She watched as he imperiously motioned these amazing women forward, one by one, with an arrogant movement of his finger. And to Beth's shock, the women obeyed, not with glares but with blushing smiles!

Why would they put up with that? Bewildered, Beth finished off her champagne. These other women were huge successes! Geniuses! She'd even recognized Sia Lane—the most famous movie star in the world!

Beth knew why she herself was here. To help her sister help those kids, and perhaps selfishly see a bit of Paris in the process. But the other women's reasons mystified her. They were all so accomplished, beautiful and well known—they couldn't need the money, could they?

And the king himself was no great shakes. Beth tilted her head, considering him from a distance. He was too skinny to be handsome. And he was rude. In West Texas, where she was from, any host worth his salt would have welcomed every guest from the moment they'd walked through his door. King or not, the man should at least have common manners.

Putting her empty flute on a passing silver tray, Beth shook her head. And what kind of man would send out for twenty women like pizza, to be delivered to him in Paris so he could choose his bride?

Even if Omar al-Maktoun was some super rich, super important ruler of a tiny Middle Eastern country she'd never heard of, he must be a serious jerk. Lucky for her, she wasn't his type. A lump lifted to her throat.

Lucky for her, she was apparently no one's type.

There was a reason why, at twenty-six, Beth was still a virgin.

Memories ambushed her without warning, punching through her with all the pain still lingering in her body, waiting to pounce at any moment of weakness. *I'm sorry, Beth. You're just too...ordinary.*

Remembering Wyatt's words, she suddenly felt like she was suffocating, gasping for breath in the too-tight cocktail dress. Blindly turning from the stuffy ballroom, she fled out the side door, where, like a miracle, she found a dark, moonlit garden in the courtyard.

Closing her eyes, she took a deep breath of the cool air, pushing away the memory of the man who'd broken her heart. She didn't need to be loved, she told herself desperately. She was helping her sister, earning money for important research. She was lucky. She'd gotten to see a bit of Paris this afternoon. The Eiffel Tower. The Arc de Triomphe. She'd sat for an hour at a sidewalk café and had a croissant and a tiny overpriced coffee, and watched the world pass by.

That was the problem. Beth wiped her eyes hard in the dark courtyard garden. Sometimes she felt, unlike her super busy sister, that all she did was watch the world pass by. Even here, in this fairy-tale Parisian mansion, surrounded by famous, glamorous people, that was all she was doing. She wasn't part of their world. Instead, she was hiding alone in the private garden.

Not entirely alone. She saw a dark shadow move amid the bare, early spring trees. A man. What was he doing out here?

She couldn't see his face, but she saw the hard, powerful grace of his stride and the tightness of his shoulders in his well-cut suit. By the hard edge of his jaw, Beth presumed he was angry. Or possibly miserable. It was hard to tell.

She wouldn't have to think about her own problems if she could help someone else with theirs. Going toward him, she said in halting, jumbled high school French, *"Excusez-moi, monsieur, est-ce que je peux vous aider—?"*

The man turned, and she gasped.

No wonder she hadn't seen him at first amid the shadows. He was black-haired, black-eyed, in a black suit. And his eyes were the blackest of all.

"What are you doing here?" His voice was a low growl, in an accent she couldn't quite place, slightly American, slightly something else.

The stranger was so handsome she lost her voice. She wished she hadn't come over. She didn't know how to talk to a man like this.

It's not his fault he's handsome, she told herself. She took a deep breath, and tried to smile. "I'm sorry. You just looked sad. I wondered if I could help at all."

His expression became so cold, it was like ice. "Who are you?"

Beth wondered if she'd offended him. Men could be so touchy, as prickly as a cactus on the outside, even when they were all sweet beneath.

At least that was her experience with her male friends, all of whom called Beth a "pal."

"My name is—" She caught herself just in time. She coughed. "Edith Farraday. *Doctor* Edith Farraday," she emphasized, trying to give him a superior, Edith-like look.

His sensual lips curved. "Ah. The child prodigy, the cancer researcher from Houston."

"Yes," she said, surprised. "You must work for the sheikh?"

That seemed to amuse him.

"Every day," he said grimly. "Why aren't you in the ballroom?"

"I got bored. And it was hot."

His gaze lowered to her red gown, which was far too small for her. Involuntarily, she blushed. She yanked up the neckline, which barely covered her generous breasts. "Yes, I know the dress doesn't fit. They didn't have anything in my size."

He frowned. "They were supposed to have every size."

Beth rolled her eyes. "Every size from zero to four. It was either this or my hoodie and jeans, and those were wet. It rained this afternoon when I was walking around the city."

He looked surprised. "You didn't rest in the hotel today like the others?"

"What, beauty sleep, so I'd look extra pretty when meeting the sheikh tonight?" She snorted. "I already know I'm not his type. And this was my only chance to see Paris. I'll be sent home tomorrow."

"How do you know?"

"Because his handlers don't know what to do with me. Plus, I've waited in that ballroom for hours, and the man still hasn't done me the great honor of crooking his mighty finger in my direction."

The man frowned. "He was rude?"

"It's fine, really," Beth said brightly. "The king's not my type, either."

The handsome stranger looked nonplussed. "How do you know? You obviously haven't done any research on him."

Beth frowned. How did the man know that? Did it show? "You got me," she admitted. "I know I should have looked him up on the internet, read up on his likes and dislikes and whatnot, but I only found out about this two days ago, and I was just too busy working before the plane left yesterday…"

He seemed shocked. "Too busy?"

"Frantic." She'd had to rush to set up the thrift shop's spring sale before her boss had grudgingly agreed to let her take her first vacation days in a year. Beth coughed. "At the lab, I mean. Super busy at the lab."

"I imagine. It's important work you're doing." The man waited, obviously expecting her to continue. But beneath the intensity of his gaze, all her carefully memorized explanations of Edith's highly technical research fled from her mind.

"Yeah. Uh. Cancer is bad."

He stared at her like she was an idiot. "Yes. I know."

"Right," she said, feeling incredibly stupid but relieved he hadn't pushed her further. She changed the subject. "So you work for the king? What are you doing out here? Why aren't you in the ballroom?"

His dark eyes glinted.

"Because I don't want to be." It struck her as the obvious answer—and yet no answer at all. A cold breeze, a vestige of the last throaty gasp of winter, blew against her bare arms and chest. Looking at him, she shivered. But not from cold.

The man towered over her, his dark suit fitting perfectly over his broad shoulders and powerful, muscular body. She'd never been so attracted to anyone like this. She felt shivery inside, overwhelmed just from being close to him. He was taller than her, bigger in every way. She felt power emanating off his body in waves. But even more dangerous than his powerful body were his eyes.

Black pools reflecting scattered bits of light, they lured her, pulled her down like a dark sea, treacherous and deep, threatening to drown her.

Beth forced herself to look away. "Well," she said unsteadily, "I should probably go inside. And wait for the king to crook his finger at me." She sighed. "It's what I'm getting paid for, after all."

"Paid?"

She looked back in surprise. "Yes. Each of the women gets a million dollars, just for showing up. And an extra million for each additional day they're invited to remain." Her lips lifted.

"Just the chance to be Queen of Samarqara should be enough," he said irritably. "A bribe shouldn't be necessary."

"Yeah, right," Beth scoffed. "I'm not sure why all these incredibly accomplished women are here, but I'm guessing the money might be a part of it." She frowned, thinking of her own sister.

"After all, even if you're famous and really good at your job, you might still need money."

"And you?" Opalescent, dappled moonlight caressed the edge of his dark brows and slash of high cheekbones. "Is that the reason you're here?"

"Of course," she whispered. She'd never had a man like this pay attention to her. What was she saying? She'd never *met* a man like this before, never, not in her whole life. He was straight out of a fairy tale, straight out of a sexy dream.

Every time this stranger looked at her, every time he spoke, her heartbeat grew faster. He was just a foot away now, and she was starting to hyperventilate. With each rapid breath, her full breasts pressed up against the overly tight sweetheart bodice of her red strapless cocktail dress. They were threatening to pop out entirely. Especially as he drew closer in the shadowy Parisian garden.

"So you're only here for money," he said flatly.

"Cancer research is expensive." Her voice trembled a little in spite of her best efforts.

"I imagine so." He stopped, looking down at her. "But I never imagined the women would be paid just to come here."

"You didn't?" Beth exhaled. He obviously

wasn't close to the sheikh, then. She was relieved. At least he wouldn't tell his boss what an
idiot Dr. Edith Farraday had looked like in the
garden, trembling and panting over a few careless words from a stranger. The real Edith would
be horrified. Or—she paused suddenly—maybe
she shouldn't make assumptions.

"Who are you to the king?" she said hesitantly.
"An attaché? A bodyguard?"

He shook his head, staring down at her incredulously. "Do you really not know?"

"Oh, are you some kind of cousin? Someone
famous? I'm sorry. I told you, I've been busy. I
was so tired I fell asleep on the plane. And today,
I've been walking around Paris…"

She was babbling, and she knew it. The man
lifted a dark eyebrow, his towering, powerful
body now just inches from her own. In the play
of moonlight and shadow, his hard, handsome
face held hers, as if she were a mystery he was
trying to solve.

Beth, a mystery? She was an open book!

Except she couldn't be, not this time. Whoever
this man was, she couldn't let him find out her
secret: that she wasn't Dr. Edith Farraday.

Until this moment, it had all just seemed like
a favor, a chance to help sick kids, and see a bit

of Paris. But the king was paying all that money for a reason. To meet Dr. Edith Farraday, not some ordinary shop girl from Houston.

And to her horror, she suddenly realized there was a legal name for what she and Edith were doing: fraud.

Nervously, Beth yanked up the stupid neckline of the red silk gown. She was in danger of falling out of it, especially as the man drew closer and her breaths became hoarse. No wonder he kept glancing down at her, then sharply looking away.

She felt ashamed, cheap and out of place. She wished she'd never come here, and was safely back at home wearing her usual baggy outfits she got for almost nothing at the thrift shop. No man ever looked at her in those for long.

"I should go," she choked out. But as she turned to go back inside the ballroom, the man's voice was husky in the shadows behind her.

"So what do you think of them?"

She turned. "Who?"

"The other women."

Beth frowned. "Why?"

"I'm curious about the opinion of someone who, as you say, doesn't have a chance with the king. If you don't, then who does?"

She narrowed her eyes. "Do you promise you won't tell the sheikh?"

"Why would you care if I did?"

"I wouldn't want to hurt anyone's chances."

He put his hand to his heart in a strangely old-fashioned gesture. "I promise I won't repeat it to anyone."

She believed him.

Reluctantly, she said, "The movie star is his obvious choice. She's the most famous beauty on earth right now."

"You're talking about Sia Lane?"

"Yeah. It's true she's incredibly beautiful. And charming." She paused. "She's also just plain mean. She harassed the flight attendants for hours on the private jet from New York, just because they didn't have the sparkling water she wanted. Then when we arrived at the hotel this morning, and the porter nearly dropped her designer suitcase, she threatened to destroy his whole family if she saw a single scratch. She's the kind of person who would kick a dog." She tilted her head. "Unless, of course, she believed the dog might be helpful to her career."

He snorted. "Go on."

Guilt made her pause. "I shouldn't have said that." She shook her head. "I'm sure she's a lovely person. Perhaps I just caught her on a bad day."

His dark eyes gave nothing away. "If she's the worst choice, who's the best?"

"Laila al-Abayyi," she said instantly. The man looked oddly pained, but she continued eagerly, "Everyone loves her. She's, like, Mother Teresa or something. And she's from Samarqara, so she knows the language and culture—"

"Who else?" he cut her off.

Confused at his sharp reaction, Beth frowned. "Bere Akinwande is beautiful and kind and smart. She'd make a fantastic queen. And there are others. Though to be honest, I don't know why any of these women would want to marry the king."

"Why?" he demanded.

"Oh, I don't know, because he's the kind of man who set up something like this to find a wife?" She rolled her eyes. "Seriously. This whole thing is just one camera short of a reality show."

"It is not easy for a man in his position to find a worthy partner," he said stiffly. He tilted his head. "Any more, I imagine, than it is easy for a lauded scientist such as yourself to take time from your important work to waste on the painful process of finding a husband the old-fashioned way."

Beth stared at him, disgruntled, then sighed as her shoulders relaxed. "You're right. Who am I to judge? At least he's paying us for our time. We're not paying *him*. I should thank him," she said cheerfully. "And I will, if I ever get the chance."

A voice came behind her.

"Dr. Farraday? What are you doing out here? You're needed in the ballroom."

One of the handlers was standing in the open doorway to the ballroom, impatiently motioning her inside. Then his eyes widened as he saw the stranger behind her. Glancing back, she saw the handsome stranger give a small shake of his head.

"Forgive me, Dr. Farraday," the handler's voice changed strangely, "but if you'd be so kind as to return to the ballroom, we'd be very grateful."

"Well, well. It seems I finally get to meet His Highness." Beth gave the handsome stranger a crooked grin. "Wish me luck."

Reaching out, he touched her bare shoulder. He looked into her eyes. His voice was deep and low, and made her shiver. "Good luck."

Beth's knees went weak. Trying to act cool,

she pulled away and said good-naturedly, "It doesn't take luck to fail. I fail at everything. I'm a pro at it."

The man frowned, puzzled. And she remembered too late: Beth had failed. Edith hadn't.

"I mean—never mind. Bye." Turning, she quickly followed the handler out of the garden.

But as she went back into the hot, crowded ballroom, and saw the sheikh sitting on the dais, she wasn't nervous anymore. She wasn't thinking about the powerful king who'd moved heaven and earth to bring together the most accomplished women in the world, merely to choose a potential bride.

Instead, Beth couldn't stop picturing the handsome stranger who'd nearly brought her to her knees with a single touch, in the moonlit shadows of a chilly Parisian garden.

In the garden, Omar stared after her, still in shock.

Was it possible that he'd just had an entire conversation with Dr. Edith Farraday without her realizing who he was?

No, surely. She had to know.

But if this was a come-on, at least it had novelty value. No woman had ever pretended not to know him before.

He'd arrogantly assumed that every woman who'd agreed to come to the *palais* tonight wished to marry him. Was it possible one didn't even know his identity? That she'd actually had so little interest in him that she hadn't bothered to read newspapers, gossip magazines, or just look him up online? It seemed incredible.

But his instincts told him that Dr. Edith Farraday hadn't been pretending. She truly had no idea who Omar was.

Just as he himself hadn't known that Khalid was paying the twenty women to come to Paris. It made sense—as the potential brides his vizier had selected were all so famous and successful—that they could hardly be expected to toss their busy schedules aside, merely for the chance to become Omar's queen. But still... It might have bruised a lesser man's ego, to realize that the chance of marrying him hadn't been enough to make women fly here from the Americas, Asia, Africa and Europe.

Which was why Khalid hadn't told him the details, obviously. He'd told his vizier to arrange it, and arrange it the man had. It was Khalid sitting in the ballroom of his Paris mansion right now, meeting each woman personally. His friend was the one who'd winnow the twenty down to the ten whom Omar would meet personally tomorrow.

Khalid was the one who'd created the criteria for choosing the twenty potential brides, and arranged for them to be brought to Paris. When Omar had first seen the list that morning, he'd been surprised to discover how career-driven and ambitious the women were. But then, hadn't he himself insisted the women must be brilliant to be his queen? Surely the woman he chose would be willing to give up her career, no matter how illustrious. What greater fate could any woman aspire to than becoming Queen of Samarqara?

There had just been one name on the list that had immediately displeased him.

"Why did you invite Laila al-Abayyi?" he'd demanded that morning. "I told you I cannot marry her."

"No," his old friend said cheerfully. "You told me you'd only marry her if all our nobles agreed she should be queen."

"Which they will not."

"The future is unknowable," Khalid said.

"Not this," Omar replied sourly. "I'm surprised

she'd even agree. How can it not be humiliating for her to compete?"

His vizier had smiled, his dark eyes glinting strangely. "Like you, sire, Miss al-Abayyi puts Samarqara's needs above her own. Her father was so insulted by your bride market plan that he was threatening to cause trouble. Then Laila announced that she approved of your plan, and that she, too, appreciates the old traditions. That calmed her father down. She accepted my invitation for diplomatic purposes, purely for the good of the nation."

For the good of the nation, plus a million dollars, it seemed.

A million dollars *per day.*

Omar set his jaw. So be it. He'd avoided marriage for long enough. He was thirty-six years old, and if he died, there was no one to inherit the throne. His only family left was Khalid, a distant cousin who wasn't even an al-Maktoun, but an al-Bayn. Omar needed an heir. He couldn't risk a return to the violent civil war that had nearly destroyed Samarqara during his grandfather's time.

Nor could he risk a love match. He'd never be such a fool again.

No. He was older now, wiser. Marriage was for

dynastic reasons only. And in the month since he'd ordered Khalid to arrange the bride market, he'd successfully avoided thinking about it. It wasn't difficult. Omar was always busy with affairs of state.

But tonight, after finishing a diplomatic meeting in the embassy, when he'd returned to the residence, he'd found himself on edge, knowing the women were there. The process had begun.

As king, Omar would only nominally make the final decision. According to the traditions of the bride market, his council would advise him of the woman they felt best suited to be his queen.

But she wouldn't just be Omar's queen. She'd also be his wife. The mother of his children. The woman in his bed and at his side. Forever.

If you marry a stranger, you could be sentencing yourself to a lifetime of misery.

Grimly, Omar pushed Khalid's warning away. The bride market had already begun, and in any event, his vizier and council could hardly choose worse for him than he'd once tried to choose for himself.

But still…

Tense and restless as he waited for the women to finish the interviews in the ballroom, he'd paced his private quarters. He'd known he couldn't meet the brides. Not yet. It wasn't protocol. But he'd found himself unable to either stay or go. So he'd gone outside in the dark, shadowy courtyard garden, trying not to think of either the future or the past.

Then he'd been interrupted by a beautiful, sensual, surprising woman. He'd been violently drawn to her, first by her incredible body, lush and ridiculously curvy in that tight dress. Then he'd been drawn by her frank, artless words. For a moment, he'd been distracted, even amused, as well as attracted.

Until even she had said that Laila, the half sister of his deceased long-ago fiancée, should be his bride.

Was there no escaping the past?

Looking up at the moonlight now, Omar felt a new chill. He'd thought the bride market would make it easier to have a clean break. Instead, tonight he was haunted more than ever by the memories of his first attempt at acquiring a bride, some fifteen years before. What a disaster that had been.

No, not a disaster. A tragedy.

One that must never happen again.

A low curse escaped him. Setting his jaw, he

followed Dr. Edith Farraday back inside the ballroom. Standing quietly against the wall so he wouldn't be noticed, he watched her from a distance, as she spoke earnestly to the vizier on the dais. Feeling his gaze, she glanced back, and their eyes met.

Then her gaze narrowed.

If she hadn't known who Omar was in the garden, she must know it now. Her look was genuinely angry—even accusing.

A hot spark went through him as Omar looked slowly over her curvy figure in that tight dress.

His relationships of the last few years—shallow, sexual and short-lived—had been mostly with ambitious, cold, wickedly skinny blondes with a cruel wit. The opposite of black-eyed Ferida al-Abayyi, the fiancée he'd lost.

Dr. Farraday was different from all of them. She was neither a cool blonde nor a sensual, sloe-eyed brunette. Her long, lustrous hair was somewhere between dishwater blond and light brown. She had a dusting of freckles over her snub nose. Her heart-shaped face was rosy, her lips full and pink, and her eyes—it was too far to see the color, but they were glaring at him now in a way he felt all the way to his groin.

But if her face was innocently wholesome, her

body was the opposite. She was a bombshell. That dress should have been illegal, he thought. Clinging to her curvaceous body, the silk whispered breathlessly that, at any moment, it might fall apart at the seams, and leave her incredible body naked and ripe for his taking. In that dress, Dr. Farraday could rule any man.

Or maybe it was just him. Looking at her in the brighter lights of the ballroom, all he could think about was taking her straight to his bed. Her skin, when he'd briefly touched her shoulder, had been even softer than silk. He could only imagine what the rest of her would feel like, naked against his own.

He took a deep, hoarse breath.

Omar could not seduce her, or any other woman here. The bride market was not about casual, easy seduction. In spite of Dr. Farraday's remark about reality shows, it was a serious tradition, not an episode of *The Bachelor*.

The only way he would have the luscious Dr. Farraday in his bed would be after marriage. And she had far more to recommend her than just mind-blowing sex appeal. Her résumé had stood out from the other nineteen, because she was a research scientist specializing in the same childhood leukemia that had killed Omar's older brother, long ago.

But if he hadn't read that, he'd have had no idea that the woman had graduated from Harvard at nineteen with both an MD and a PhD in biochemistry. At twenty-six, she already led a team in Houston, doing bleeding-edge research. Edith Farraday rarely left the lab, he'd heard.

Someone like that should have been daunting, cold, formidable. But Dr. Edith Farraday didn't act like her résumé. She was so different in person, Omar thought, that she almost seemed an entirely different woman.

She was warm, kind, self-effacingly funny. Even though she was different from his usual type, he was overwhelmingly attracted to her. Or maybe it was *because* she was so different.

Omar blinked when he heard the whispers in the ballroom suddenly explode, as a low rumble of shocked noise swirled around him. He'd been recognized by the other women in the ballroom. Without a word, he turned and disappeared back into the garden, and then to his private quarters in the residence.

But at the end of the evening, he stood alone in the upstairs salon, watching through the window as, below him, all twenty of the would-be brides climbed into limousines waiting to take them back to the luxurious, five-star Campania Hotel on the avenue Montaigne.

"The things I do for you, Your Highness." His vizier's voice came behind him. "Are you ready yet to just be sensible and marry the al-Abayyi girl?"

Not dignifying that question with a response, Omar turned. "You've made your decision which ten will be sent home?"

"It wasn't easy." Khalid paused. "Except for the last one. I barely spoke ten words to her before I knew she wasn't your type."

He was speaking of Dr. Edith Farraday, Omar realized, and said irritably, "I don't have a type. Why does everyone think I have a type?"

"Because you do."

Omar replied, annoyed, "And Dr. Edith Farraday isn't it?"

"Beautiful girl, but a little too common for you, I thought. She's put on weight since her last published photographs, too. Her dress looked outrageously tight." Khalid blinked. "Am I wrong?"

Omar stared back out the window. He watched as Dr. Farraday got into the last limo. She looked back up wistfully at the mansion, as if she knew that she'd never come back, as if trying to remember everything.

It doesn't take luck to fail, she'd said. *I fail at everything. I'm a pro at it.*

What a strange comment for a world-famous genius to make, he thought. Because she hadn't yet found a cure for biphenotypic acute leukemia, all her accomplishments meant nothing?

But she would understand, as few could, how it felt to be single-minded in pursuit of one's duty—for her, curing cancer, for him, the responsibility of leading a nation.

Common, Khalid had called her. And he was right. Edith Farraday didn't have the imperious edge, the formality, the arrogance of a queen. She was unorthodox, a little undignified, and yet...

And yet...

Omar wanted her. Suddenly, and beyond reason.

No. A pulse of danger went through him. Any of the other women would be a safer choice, even Laila al-Abayyi. Because he could not, dare not allow emotion into this choice. Never again. The cost of loving, of wanting, was too high—

it brought destruction, not just on him but upon innocent people.

In spite of knowing this, though, Omar gripped the edge of the translucent curtain as he watched the limo drive out past the gate. Dr. Farraday had warmed him in the garden. Warmed?

The image passed through his mind of her voluptuous figure, her full breasts pushing up against the ruched silk, fighting a battle for modesty and losing. Her eyes sparkling in furious indignation as she'd glared at him across the ballroom, unconsciously licking her full, pink lips—

A rush of heat went through him, straight to his groin. He nearly groaned aloud.

But he could not seduce her. He could not even kiss her. Not unless and until he formally proclaimed her his bride on the steps of his royal palace in Samarqara.

And he could never choose Dr. Farraday as queen. Khalid was right. She was too open, too honest, too sexy. Not at all appropriate. So he should send her away. At once, if not sooner.

"Sire?" his vizier asked. "Shall I send the Farraday woman home?"

But as Omar turned, all he could think about was how seeing her in the cold, dark garden had been like seeing the bright, warm sun after a long-dead winter. And he heard himself growl, "One more night."

CHAPTER TWO

SO THAT WAS THAT.

The next morning, when Beth heard the hard knock at the door, she lifted her backpack to her shoulder and looked at her luxurious hotel suite one last time.

In the soft morning light, the suite looked magical, like a princess's bedchamber, with a fireplace and four-poster bed, a wrought-iron balcony edged with pink flowers, and a white marble bathroom bigger than her whole studio apartment back home. She'd taken pictures to show her friends back at the thrift shop.

Outside, the morning sun was soft over Paris. Beneath the Eiffel Tower, white neoclassical buildings glowed as pink as frosted cupcakes. She saw birds flying over the avenue Montaigne, soaring over the fresh blue sky.

Beth looked at her hoodie and jeans, which had been freshly cleaned and pressed by the hotel staff overnight. Unlike the other brides, she'd traveled light, with only a backpack, which was now stuffed with her neatly folded silk cocktail dress from last night. The king's staff had made it clear they didn't want it, and she knew someone at the thrift shop certainly would.

She took a deep breath. She was glad to be returning home. She didn't belong here, in this glamorous world.

Her place was in her Houston neighborhood, in her studio walk-up apartment near the community college, where she'd been taking part-time classes until her heartbreak over Wyatt made her drop out. Since then, her part-time job at the thrift shop had become full-time, and she biked to work each morning, rain or shine, because she couldn't afford car insurance, much less a car. She sometimes worked extra jobs to make ends meet, and in her spare time, she volunteered at the local soup kitchen, the food pantry and the senior center. That was the life she knew.

But Beth wanted to remember this Paris adventure, down to the last moment. Because she knew it would never happen again.

After her shock last night, realizing she'd been talking to the actual king the whole time in the garden, she'd expected to be awake all night, agonizing about what an idiot she'd been. Instead, she'd slept like a log, wrapped in soft cotton sheets that had a thread count higher than her paycheck. After a long, hot shower that morning in the palatial bathroom, she'd eaten breakfast in bed, brought by room service, with toasted baguettes called *tartines* slathered with butter and marmalade, and fresh, flaky chocolate croissants that melted literally like butter in her mouth, and drunk fresh-squeezed orange juice and strong coffee with fresh cream.

But her time as a princess was over. When her phone buzzed an hour before, she hadn't even bothered to check the message. She already knew what it would say: she was being sent home.

Now, the knock. She hesitated, staring at the door. Once she answered it, she knew she'd find a servant waiting to escort her to the minibus that would take her back to the airport, along with the rest of the rejected ten. How could it be otherwise, when after criticizing a famous movie star, Beth had actually insulted the king as well—right to his handsome, sensual face?

Beth flinched, remembering how stupid she'd felt when she'd finally spoken to the man on the throne, only to discover it was just a regular chair, and the man was just a vizier and that only the ten women to make the next cut would have the honor of actually meeting the king in person.

"But where is he now?" she'd asked as a creeping suspicion built inside her.

The vizier replied with a disapproving stare, "His Highness is busy with affairs of state."

And then, like a flash, Beth had known.

Why aren't you in the ballroom?

Because I don't want to be.

Who else but the king could choose whether he wished to attend such a gala in his own residence? Who else could be so arrogant, wear such a well-cut suit and be able to lounge in the residence's garden at his leisure? She remembered the handler's shocked look, and the handsome stranger's small shake of the head.

You must work for the sheikh? she'd asked. Amused, he'd replied, *Every day.*

As she stood beside the vizier in the ballroom, her horrible suspicion built to certainty. Then she'd felt someone's gaze behind her. Turning, she'd seen the handsome stranger himself now beside the door, watching her across the ballroom with cool, inscrutable eyes. And she'd remembered her own embarrassing words. *I don't know why any of these women would want to marry the king... This whole thing is just one camera short of a reality show.*

At any time, the king could have revealed himself and stopped her. Instead, he'd just let her carry on making a fool of herself. Angry and humiliated, Beth had glared at him for a moment in the ballroom. Then she'd turned away, cheeks burning. When her interview with the vizier was finally over, the king was nowhere in sight.

She told herself she was relieved she'd never see him again. Just being near him had done crazy things to her. She shivered, her cheeks even now flooding with color at the memory.

He should have had the common decency to tell her who he was, straightaway. The man had no manners whatsoever. And if she ever saw him again—

The knock pounded again on her door, even harder and louder. Gripping the straps of her backpack, Beth answered the door with a sigh. "All right, I'm coming—"

Standing in the doorway, she saw King Omar himself, dressed from head to toe in regal sheikh's robes.

Her jaw dropped as she took an involuntary step back. His black eyes pierced her. His powerful body seemed to fill every inch of the doorway as he looked down at her grimly.

"So. You know who I am."

It was a statement, not a question. Trembling, she nodded. All her earlier ideas of pointing out his bad manners flew straight out the window. Her knees were trembling, and all she could think was that he'd discovered she wasn't Edith. Why else would the king himself come to see her, rather than just having his servants escort her onto the Minibus of Shame?

"Why are you here?" she whispered through dry lips.

"I have good news and bad news, Dr. Farraday." His husky voice was faintly mocking. "The good news is—you're coming with me."

Where? To jail? "Then what's the bad news?" she blurted out.

"I'm afraid word has gotten out." He paused, and fear rushed through her body, until he continued smoothly, "Paparazzi have surrounded this hotel. I'm here to escort you and the others out the back." He motioned to a servant hovering behind him in the hotel hallway. "Saad will get your luggage."

She indicated the backpack on her shoulder.

"This is all I have. This, and the clothes on my back."

The king's dark eyes flickered over her. "I will send for more clothes for you."

Beth shook her head in confusion. "It's not necessary—"

"Isn't it?" His gaze lingered over her oversize gray hoodie and baggy jeans as she stood in the hotel suite. She suddenly wished she had something nicer to wear. But that didn't make sense. If he hadn't learned her real identity, which it seemed he hadn't, what did she care what the king thought of her as he took her to the airport?

And yet, somehow, she did care. Remembering how his darkly intense eyes had traced down her bare throat last night to her overflowing breasts, she blushed. Last night, it had felt like she'd wandered into a romantic dream, with the two of them alone in a moonlit Parisian garden.

Dream? No. He'd made a fool of her.

The third man to do that, she thought, and her heart lifted to her throat. "I don't understand," she said stiltedly. "The good news is that you're taking me to the airport personally?"

"No." His dark eyebrows lowered. "Back to the mansion."

Beth frowned, bewildered. "All twenty of us are going back?"

"Only the ten who are staying another night."

Beth stared at him.

"I made it to the top ten?" she whispered. It was so unexpected she hugged the thought close to her chest.

The sheikh frowned at her. "You are not pleased?"

Beth's feelings were so mixed up she hardly knew how she felt. "Um...are you sure it's not a mistake?"

He snorted, then tilted his head, considering her. "You are different."

A flutter went through her heart. "I am?"

"Yes." Their eyes locked, and his gaze electrified her body, from her fingertips to her toes and everywhere between. "So will you come?"

No. She had to say no. She'd gotten the million dollars for Edith. Only a fool would press her luck—

"Of course," she blurted out.

A slow-rising smile lifted his sensual lips. "This way, if you please, Dr. Farraday."

Dr. Farraday. As Beth walked with him down the hotel hallway, his servant following behind, her heart fell back to her canvas sneakers.

Remembering how angry she'd been at him for not disclosing his identity in the garden, she felt ashamed. Talk about the pot calling the kettle black.

And if he found out—*when* he found out—

Oh, this was getting dangerously complicated. She'd never imagined he'd choose her to stay another night, not in a million years!

But one more day would mean another million for Edith's research. Then tomorrow, she'd go home for sure. Surely she could fake it for another twenty-four hours. No one the wiser, and no one hurt.

But as she left the Paris hotel, going out into the bright sunlight where the limos waited, Beth barely noticed the paparazzi with their lifted cameras and shouted questions, and the bodyguards holding them back. Looking up at the handsome, powerful billionaire king beside her, she felt equal parts intoxicated—and afraid.

For the first time since she could remember, she'd been chosen for something. The king didn't think Beth was *ordinary*. He thought she was different. That she was special.

The thought warmed her all over. Until she remembered he hadn't chosen Beth.

He'd chosen Edith.

* * *

"You collected the Farraday woman from her hotel suite? Yourself?"

Khalid's voice was shocked.

"I had no choice. She wouldn't answer the phone." Standing in the grand salon back at his Paris residence, Omar looked out irritably at the hordes of paparazzi now clustered outside the tall wrought-iron gates. Someone had tipped off the press about the bride market. Who? He wondered grimly. One of his scorned would-be brides? Or perhaps one of the ten he'd kept?

Perhaps Sia Lane, the movie star Dr. Farraday had called "downright mean," had decided to hedge her bets with a little more publicity?

Whoever'd done it, the story had exploded instantly. It was too juicy for the media to treat it otherwise, with the famous playboy king of a small Middle Eastern kingdom bringing women from around the globe to choose a queen. The story was making news everywhere.

It's one camera short of a reality show, Dr. Farraday had said. She was right.

Dr. Edith Farraday. Just thinking of her warmed Omar. She'd looked shocked in the hotel suite two hours before, as if she'd never expected to be chosen.

Perhaps he'd been wrong to choose her. But how could he send away the one woman who was different—the one who made his body come alive? He'd told himself that all his initial concern was overcautious. So he was attracted to her. What of it?

Attraction wasn't love, or the kind of mind-blowing lust that caused civilizations to crumble.

He just wanted her. And there was some mystery in her that he couldn't quite understand. Her lovely expression, frank and honest, had a way of changing, becoming guarded. As if she were hiding something from him. But what?

Today, he'd find out.

Then he'd send her home tomorrow.

"You shouldn't have escorted her yourself. It's not how it's supposed to be done," Khalid continued, obviously disgruntled. "If you escort one lady from her hotel suite, you must do the same for the rest. Otherwise it gives the appearance of favoritism."

Omar dropped the curtain abruptly and turned to face the other man. "Dr. Farraday *is* my favorite," he said bluntly.

His vizier's expression soured. "But surely, she isn't as beautiful or elegant as—"

"Say Laila al-Abayyi's name, and I'm sending you straight back to Samarqara."

The other man paused, and his mouth snapped shut. Then he ventured, "Dr. Farraday does not seem to have the same polish as the others. Perhaps she has spent too much time in her lab. The brief time I interviewed her, she was far too artless and frank in her speech. The council would not approve of her obvious lack of diplomacy."

Thinking of Dr. Farraday's casual, accidental insults to him in the garden, Omar was forced to agree. He said shortly, "She amuses me. Nothing more."

"Ah." His vizier's face looked relieved.

"I collected Dr. Farraday from her suite because it was expedient. And I did not escort her to her room here."

Although heaven knew he'd wanted to.

That morning, the other nine women had all rushed from their hotel rooms immediately after the phone call informing them they'd made the top ten. They'd clustered together, filling up the first limousine. Leaving Omar alone with the luscious Dr. Farraday in the second limo.

Sitting beside her on the drive from the hotel back to his Paris mansion, he'd been aware of her, so aware. It had taken all his willpower to make polite conversation with her, when his mind had been on something else altogether. He'd wanted to pull up the privacy screen to block out the view of the driver and bodyguard in front, so he could push her against the soft calfskin leather of the wide back seat, pull off that ridiculously baggy sweatshirt and discover the delights of the amazing curves she'd flaunted last night.

"Very well, sire…" his vizier said haltingly. "Of course you must enjoy your amusements in the midst of a serious business. So long as you consider your actual choice wisely. It took some trouble to bring these women to Paris."

"Some money, you mean," Omar said coldly. "I heard about the payments."

"You are displeased with my method?" Khalid shook his head. "It's nothing to your fortune. A mere rounding error."

He glowered. "That isn't the point."

"Then what is?" His friend looked stubborn. "A bride price is part of the tradition, you know that. Isn't it better for the payment to go to the brides themselves, rather than the antiquated custom of paying their fathers?"

Omar could hardly argue with that. "Of course," he bit out. "But still…"

"Still?"

He could hardly explain that it had hurt his pride. His friend would say, with some cause, that it was well deserved. He growled, "I never gave you authorization."

"You just told me to arrange it. And made it quite clear you didn't wish to be bothered with the details."

Another thing Omar could not argue with. He scowled.

Khalid's eyebrows rose. "And surely you approve of the results. All these women are beautiful and brilliant. Just as you commanded."

"Yes," he was forced to concede. Based on their pictures and resumes alone, they were more accomplished than he'd ever imagined. "Assuming they are willing to give up those brilliant careers to be Queen of Samarqara."

"And why would they not?" Khalid replied indignantly. "Being Samarqara's Queen is surely the greatest honor any woman could imagine."

Omar hesitated. He'd assumed the same thing himself, and yet suddenly he was not so sure.

He himself had been forced to leave college at twenty-one and ascend the throne, casting all personal ambitions aside after his father had died. But he'd known that would be his fate from the day his older brother had died. As the only heir of a country that could still remember the horrors of civil war, Omar had always known he must put his country's needs above his own. Any man of honor would have done the same.

And so it was with this marriage. After the awful tragedy with Ferida, he'd put marriage off indefinitely. Until, in New York on a recent diplomatic visit, he'd seen an elderly couple walking down Fifth Avenue. They hadn't been special, or rich, or beautiful. But they'd held hands tenderly as they walked together. The man had gazed down lovingly at his wife, and she at him. And Omar had felt a sharp pain in his throat.

He did not expect that kind of devotion. Why would he? His own parents' marriage had been a disaster. Selfishly trying to find love only brought pain, or worse—death.

Coming home, Omar had ordered his vizier to begin the preparations for the bride market. He wanted this marriage finished. Done. Before he ever let himself again be tempted by something so destructive as a foolish dream.

He would take a bride who felt the same. A woman who'd put others first, as Omar did. Who would see the sacrifice not just as a burden, but an honor.

At least most of the time.

"One of the ten women would see it as a greater honor than the rest," his vizier said slowly. "She has no other career than to be a dutiful daughter and the pride of her people. She already speaks our language, knows our customs—"

Omar cut him off with a glare. Setting his jaw, he said with some restraint, "Bring the ten in now."

His vizier's jaw tightened, and he looked as if he were biting back words. Then he bowed and went to open the door to the grand salon. Outside, in the elegant hallway, ten women were waiting.

Eight of them, he'd meet for the first time. The ninth, he was trying to avoid. The tenth, he could hardly stop thinking about. He'd speak with Dr. Farraday last. She would be his dessert. His whipped cream. His cherry on—

Realizing he was starting to get aroused, he stopped the thought cold.

Because his vizier was right. As much as he desired Edith Farraday, she seemed an unlikely queen. Aside from her lack of tact, it was almost impossible that she'd be willing to give up her life as a research scientist. It was obviously her obsession, in spite of her strange reluctance to talk about it. And Laila was a nonstarter.

So he needed to seriously consider the other eight. Any one of them could be an appropriate queen, one the council would approve of, and if he were lucky, one he could admire and respect. So, for the rest of the afternoon and evening, he'd meet with each woman privately, for as long or short a time as he deemed appropriate.

But the plans for today had been that he'd get to know his ten potential brides by touring the sights of Paris with each of them separately. That would be more difficult with paparazzi outside the gate, holding up their cameras as reporters yelled obnoxious questions. Anywhere they tried to go, the paparazzi would follow.

But at least it would not last long. Tomorrow morning, he'd send five more women home. The remaining five, the true contenders, would return with him to Samarqara to meet the council in preparation for the main event: the bride market itself.

Now, standing beside the banquet table, Omar watched as the ten women entered the grand salon of his Paris mansion.

Nine women looked like carbon copies, though all in different shades and colors—classically beautiful, slender, elegant, tall and perfectly dressed in sleek designer outfits.

Then there was the last one, shorter than the rest, and rounder. Her cheeks were pink, her eyes bright, her light brown hair wavy and wild. Against his will, his eyes traced over her. Her curves were invisible beneath the baggy hoodie and jeans. But his body stirred, becoming instantly hard.

Why her?

Omar couldn't answer the question, even to himself.

As the women entered the grand salon one by one, he stood near the end of the banquet table in his full sheikh's robes, making eye contact with each one, giving each a welcoming nod, as he did during any other diplomatic endeavor. The women each smiled, or preened, or nodded back coolly, in their turn.

And in spite of his best efforts to be open-minded, he found himself unimpressed, in spite of all their obvious charms. He was bored by them, beauty, success and all.

Except for the woman who came in last, looking pink-cheeked and miserable, hanging in the back of the salon. The one who wouldn't meet his eyes.

Dr. Edith Farraday. And again he felt it, along with his powerful attraction—that mystery he couldn't solve. As Khalid had pointed out, Omar had already made it clear by his attentions that she was his favorite. So why did she hang back, behind the rest? Why did her hazel eyes look haunted and guilty, as if she'd committed some crime?

He didn't like ambiguity. He wanted her mystery solved. Now. Tonight.

And in a perfect world, he would have solved the mystery with them both naked in bed.

"Welcome," his vizier said formally, spreading his arms wide in his robes. "I will be presenting each of you in turn to His Highness, the King of Samarqara. Please—" he indicated the tables full of drinks and lavish food "—until your name is called, please feel free to mingle and relax."

Omar sat down at the chair at the end of the table. Standing beside him, Khalid motioned to the first woman.

"Miss Sia Lane."

The beautiful blonde came forward and gave a slightly ironic nod, then at his motioned invitation, sat down in the chair beside him. His vizier said gravely, "Sire, Miss Lane is a very well-known actress from Los Angeles, California."

"Pleased to meet you, Your Highness," she said.

"And you, Miss Lane." It wasn't surprising that his vizier had chosen her to make the cut. She was the world's most famous beauty, and her chilly glamour reminded him of many of his past mistresses. On paper, Sia Lane would make an excellent bride, a prestigious new member to join any royal family, as when Grace Kelly had become Princess of Monaco or Meghan Markle became Duchess of Sussex.

But when Omar reached out to shake Sia Lane's hand, her skin felt cold and dry. He felt nothing, in spite of her beauty. He dropped her hand.

"Welcome," he said gravely. "Thank you for coming to meet me."

"My pleasure," the blonde murmured, fluttering her eyelashes at him, arrogantly sure of her own appeal. He recalled Dr. Farraday's tart assessment: *She's the kind of person who would kick a dog, unless, of course, she believed the dog might be helpful to her career.*

Taking his wry smile for praise, the movie star tilted her chin in a practiced move he'd seen in her films. They spoke briefly, then he dismissed her with a polite nod. She seemed almost surprised, as if she'd expected to be proclaimed his queen, here and now.

Khalid called the next woman forward. "Dr. Bere Akinwande."

"Your Highness," she said politely, with a short bow. Speaking with her as she sat beside him, he thought Dr. Edith Farraday's character assessment was correct once again. She seemed an excellent choice to be his queen—a doctor, she spoke six languages, and had been nominated for a Nobel prize. She spoke earnestly of the work she was doing, the difference it could make in the world, and thanked him twice for the "donation" he'd given her. She did not try to flirt. She'd clearly come for the money, but then—he thought again of Dr. Farraday's important research—could he blame her for that?

Dr. Bere Akinwande was accomplished, intelligent and pretty, but when he shook her hand, again, he felt nothing.

"Laila al-Abayyi," his vizier intoned, his voice solemn.

Omar repressed his feelings as he was formally introduced to the young Samarqari heiress. Looking in her lovely face, he saw the same black eyes, the same dark beauty, the same masses of long, shiny dark hair that he remembered seeing in her half sister Ferida, fifteen years ago. Ferida, whom he'd arrogantly demanded as his bride, before it had all ended in death and sand—

Dropping her hand, he said shortly, "Goodbye."

"Goodbye?" Laila said, looking bewildered at being cut off when she'd been in the middle of shyly praising the improvements of his rule.

"You may return to your room. I will not meet with you later."

"You—you won't?"

"I thank you for your intercessions with your father. But any further contact between us would be unwelcome."

Laila turned pale. "Oh. I—I see…" With a hurt glance toward the vizier, the brunette fled the salon.

"Sire," his vizier said in a low voice for his ears alone, "that was unconscionable—"

"She should not be here." Omar's jaw was hard as stone as he turned on him. "Do you understand? I will not marry her. Ever."

His vizier's eyes narrowed, then he gave an

unsteady nod. Turning, he called the next potential bride's name.

Omar was glad of the chance to calm the rapid, sickening beat of his heart, as he offered the same polite courtesy to the next woman, then the next, expressing gratitude for their visit to Paris. They always thanked him in return, smiling, their eyes lingering appreciatively over his face and body. So far, so good.

But after that, he started to feel like a bank manager, not a king. The entrepreneur from Germany, tossing her hair, explained in detail that she was seeking investors for her tech start-up. The gymnast from Brazil, smiling flirtatiously, told him of her desire to build an expensive new training facility in São Paulo. The senator from California, her gaze falling to his mouth, wished to discuss favorable trade negotiations for her state's dairy farmers. And so on.

Many of the women had clearly come to Paris to pursue their career goals, as Dr. Farraday had. Only a few of them seemed blindly ready to toss their important careers away for a Cinderella fantasy that had little to do with the rigors of actual leadership.

He wasn't sure which was worse.

But he was always aware of the one woman

in the background, standing by the wall, hovering in the corners, moving in the shadows. One woman who, in spite of her obvious determination to be invisible, shone out for him like no other.

Finally, his vizier's voice said grudgingly, "And finally, sire, Dr. Edith Farraday. A well-known cancer researcher from Houston, Texas."

Watching her as she came forward, Omar could have sworn that she flinched at the sound of her own name. Why? Was she so unwilling to meet with him?

Her earlier words came floating back: *I don't know why any of these women would want to marry the sheikh.*

Was it possible that, even though he was so attracted to her, she wasn't attracted to him at all?

No, surely not. Women always fell at his feet. He was the King of Samarqara, billionaire, absolute ruler of a wealthy kingdom.

But then, was Dr. Edith Farraday, child prodigy, high-minded scientist, the sort of person to be impressed by money and power? For all he knew, she had a boyfriend back home. An ordinary but perfectly satisfying man who was content to let her be the superstar, while he cooked her dinners and rubbed her feet. She might find that sort of man much more appealing to her lifestyle than some playboy king who, until this very moment, had been unable and unwilling to commit to anything beyond his own rule.

It was a discomfiting thought.

"Oh. Hello again," Edith said uneasily, her eyes darting to the right and left, as if she felt guilty. Guilty?

Was there a boyfriend?

The question set him on edge.

"It's a pleasure to finally be properly introduced," Omar said gravely. He looked over her outfit, the exact same hoodie and jeans that she'd worn when he'd knocked on her hotel room door that morning, and tilted his head curiously. "Did the new wardrobe I had sent to your room not meet with your approval?"

"The clothes are beautiful, thank you," she said, her eyes guarded.

"And yet you are not wearing them."

"They really weren't necessary. I'm only going to be here one more day."

"And a night," he pointed out.

She looked away evasively. "I suppose. But I knew if I wore them, your people couldn't return them to the store. So I didn't touch them."

Omar stared at her incredulously. "You're worried about the cost?"

She actually blushed. "I suppose it's silly but… I don't like taking advantage of people…"

Then her voice abruptly cut off. Her cheeks turned from pink to bright red.

He frowned, puzzled by her reaction. "You're not taking advantage. You're my guest. I want you to be comfortable."

"Oh, I am," she said in a strangled voice. She tried to smile, but her face was stiff and awkward.

"Is there some reason you wish to rush back to Houston?" He watched her. "A boyfriend back home?"

Her eyes flashed wide. "What?" she said quickly. "No!"

Omar relaxed. "So you miss your work at the lab, then."

"Oh. Yes. Of course I do." She paused, then blurted, "I'd hoped to see more of Paris today. But I was just told that we won't be allowed to leave the mansion this afternoon?"

"An unfortunate circumstance, with all the paparazzi outside the gate."

She bit her lip. "I know I'm being silly, it's

just… I didn't get a chance to see the Louvre yet, or climb the Eiffel Tower. The line for tickets was too long. I was hoping…" Squaring her shoulders, she shook her head. "Ah, well, it doesn't matter."

"The Louvre? You like art?"

"I wanted to see the *Mona Lisa*. Who doesn't?"

"You've never seen it?" It seemed strange she'd never been to Paris before. He was sure the other women had visited many times, for school trips or family vacations, or, as in the case of Laila al-Abayyi, because their families owned lavish penthouses with a view of the Seine.

Dr. Farraday was indeed very busy in the lab, it seemed. Totally and utterly dedicated to her cause since she was a teenager.

Not a bad quality for a queen, an important part of him argued. Sadly it was the part of him that wanted her in his bed.

But Dr. Farraday had a quiet beauty, in a way that perhaps a man wouldn't notice right away, especially in those baggy jeans and hoodie, with her hair pulled up in a ponytail. She wasn't even wearing makeup.

As accustomed as Omar was to women constantly trying to get his attention, it was strange indeed to meet a woman who seemed determined to evade it. In fact, if he hadn't seen her in that tight red dress yesterday, he might have easily overlooked her even now.

Surely not. Was he so shallow as that?

When she didn't sit down beside him, Omar rose abruptly to his feet. "Thank you for coming to Paris to meet me, Dr. Farraday."

"No problem." She gave him a crooked smile. "Thanks for the two million for cancer research."

He couldn't look away from her smile, or the way her eyes suddenly sparkled beneath the chandeliers. "You must tell me about your latest scientific breakthroughs."

The smile on her face dropped away. Why? Because he'd reminded her of the important cancer research she was neglecting to be here? She gave an awkward laugh. "I, uh, don't like to talk about it. Most people find the details very dull."

"Try me. I'm not a scientist, but I do keep up on developments in the search for the cure for biphenotypic acute leukemia."

Her voice was a croak. "You do?"

Omar gave a short nod. "Perhaps later, while discussing your research, we could also discuss an additional donation from my country's charitable fund."

There. The perfect bait to make any scientist talk.

And yet she still didn't.

"Uh—maybe later," she managed. She glanced around the salon, then leaned forward to whisper, "Why did you really want me to stay in Paris? For an insider's opinion on your potential brides? Or just for comic relief?"

"Maybe I like your company," he said. "I enjoyed talking to you in the garden."

"You should have told me who you were…" Then she shook her head. "Never mind. It doesn't matter."

"No, you're right," he said softly. "I should have told you. I was just surprised. I'm not accustomed to people not recognizing me."

"That's funny. I'm used to being invisible. To everyone." As their eyes locked, her face looked strangely vulnerable. "Why did you choose me?"

She didn't know how beautiful she was, he realized. How could any woman as beautiful, incredible and important as Dr. Edith Farraday have such a low opinion of her own value?

She hadn't known who Omar was when they'd met in the garden last night. That had seemed strange enough. But it seemed Dr. Farraday didn't know who *she* was, either. Or how truly amazing she was.

Even now, with his vizier and servants and the other would-be brides watching their every move, all Omar could think about was how much he liked her. Perhaps she could be taught diplomacy, and she'd give up her lab and—

He stopped the thought cold. His body was willing to argue anything that would allow him to seduce her.

"I wanted you to stay because I'm curious," he said.

Her expression became guarded. "Curious? About what?"

"About you," he said honestly, even as he told himself he couldn't have her. She was too consumed by her important work. She would make a poor queen, if forced to quit her research, and she'd be desperately unhappy. She was absolutely forbidden to him. He was sending her home tomorrow.

And that, of course, made him want her even more. He ground his teeth.

"Sire." His vizier appeared at his elbow. "It is time for your first date."

"Yes." With an inward sigh, Omar gave Dr. Farraday a brief, respectful bow. "Until later."

She gave a brief smile. "Of course. Good luck."

She was wishing him luck? On his dates with other women?

"You truly are a mystery." The last low word hung between them, intimately, like a promise. He held out his hand.

She hesitated, then took it.

As their palms touched, Omar felt an electric shock against his skin, passing through muscle and blood and bone. When he enfolded her smaller hand in his own, his whole body came alive.

He dropped her hand. And the question echoed through his heart like a curse: Why her? Why did his body react to the one woman he already knew he could not make his queen? The universe had a strange sense of humor.

No, not strange, Omar thought grimly as he watched Dr. Farraday depart the salon. His jaw was tight. *Vengeful.*

Beth waited in her room all afternoon, but the king didn't come. She read books, paced around her elegant room, left frantic messages for her sister in Houston. She ate lunch brought to her room on a silver tray. She changed into one of the new dresses he'd had sent to her, nervously watching the hours tick by.

But he never came.

Good, Beth tried to tell herself. She glanced at the gilded antique clock on the fireplace mantel. Ten o'clock at night. Obviously, his other dates had gone well. Perhaps he'd already chosen one of the other nine as his bride.

She told herself she was relieved. She couldn't continue this farce for much longer. It was horrifying, exhausting, even terrifying, to pretend to be someone she was not.

Beth shuddered, remembering the moment the king had casually mentioned that he "kept up on developments" in biphenotypic acute leukemia!

Her cheeks burned. All they needed was one in-depth scientific conversation and he'd realize that Beth knew nothing at all about it. She'd tried to memorize the scientific jargon, honestly she had. But her brain just blocked it out.

Even in elementary school, Edith had been the genius, not her. So Beth had simply stopped trying. Let her twin sister be the one to excel in academics. She would be good at something else.

The trouble was, at twenty-six, Beth was still trying to figure out what that something else was. She was starting to suspect it might be nothing.

She should be glad that Omar had forgotten about her. Beth would be able to go home in triumph, knowing Edith now had two million for research. And she didn't even need to feel guilty about coming here under false pretenses, as long as the king chose a better bride than Beth. Which was basically any of the other nine women—except Sia Lane.

For some reason she couldn't fathom, she felt protective of the king. It was ridiculous. Handsome, powerful and rich, he was the last person on earth who needed Beth's protection. And yet something about his gentle nature suggested a kind heart, beneath all the arrogance and ferocity. Some dark past, Beth thought. As if he'd been hurt before.

And she already knew he deserved better than that cold-hearted, beautiful, two-faced movie star as his wife.

She paced over the white fluffy rug on the pale gray floor. The bedroom she'd been assigned in his royal residence was even more luxurious than the hotel suite on the avenue Montaigne. Glamorous and sleek, with Art Deco flourishes, the pretty, feminine room was silver and white except for the brilliant splashes of pink and red provided by the flowers in the silver vase on the vanity table.

Beth stopped. If she could only be sure he would choose a wife who would love him, someone obviously worthy, like Laila al-Abayyi! Then she could leave tomorrow with a clear conscience, if not a joyful heart.

Seeing herself in the full-length mirror, she caught her breath. All the time she'd spent getting ready tonight for a so-called date had made her look…different. She wasn't wearing her usual baggy clothes. Nor was she packed like a sausage into a too-tight gown.

The clothes he'd arranged to be sent to her room were—perfect.

Beth didn't have an easy body to fit. She was petite, and unlike her totally skinny, size two sister—Edith often forgot to eat in the lab whereas Beth had never seen a slice of cake she didn't like. Beth's waist was small, but she was cursed with big breasts and big hips. The modern, straight-shaped styles just looked like oversize sacks on her.

But now, staring at the new gown that was fitted to her shape, Beth came closer to the mirror, staring at herself in amazement. The dress was a deep sapphire, in soft silk. She'd brushed out her frizzy light brown waves and made her hair glossy and straight, hanging to the middle of her back. She'd experimented with the boxes of brand-new makeup in the en suite bathroom. She'd put on eyeliner, mascara, lipstick. It was the first time she'd worn makeup in a year, since the night her boyfriend announced he was breaking up with her for a girl who was, in his description, "more interesting."

Wyatt's harsh breakup had been the second time a boyfriend had told Beth she wasn't desirable. Against such evidence, she'd decided that, in addition to not being good at school, she apparently wasn't good at relationships, either. At least not romantic ones. So rather than risk being hurt again, for the last year, she'd just opted out.

Now, Beth looked at herself. Her hazel eyes glittered dangerously, lined in black. Her lips looked glamorous, full and red. Her hips thrust forward, forced by the angle of her designer stiletto heels.

There was a brief hard knock at the door.

"Wait," Beth said, whirling around.

But too late. The door pushed open, and Omar stood in the doorway, dressed in his regal sheikh's robes that made him look almost too sexy to believe he was even real. His black eyes widened as he stared at her, standing in the dress in front of the mirror.

Her cheeks burned with indignation. "You should have waited a minute before you flung open the door like that. You might have walked in to find me naked!"

Her voice faltered as his dark eyes narrowed at her words. He wasn't touching her. He was on the other side of the bedroom. So why did she feel such a blast of heat from his gaze? Why did waves of awareness—hunger—suddenly wash through her like an earthquake?

"You are right," Omar said in a low voice, his gaze slowly tracing over her. "You look…."

For a moment, beneath his hot gaze, Beth couldn't breathe. When he didn't finish the sentence, she managed with a crooked smile, "Weird, right? I look weird?"

His voice was low. "You look beautiful."

With an intake of breath, she met his gaze. "I do?"

He came forward. His black eyes reflected the moonlight from the window as he looked down at her, his tall, powerful body just inches from hers.

"More than beautiful." Reaching out, he cupped

her cheek and said huskily, "You look tempting beyond belief."

As she felt his touch against her skin, all rational thought disappeared from her brain. His gaze fell to her lips, and a pulse of electricity went through her body. Her knees went weak.

He turned away. Reaching into the large wardrobe, he selected a new, faux fur coat, and wrapped it around her bare shoulders in an old-fashioned, almost courtly gesture.

"Are we going somewhere?" she breathed, still dizzy at his nearness.

Silently, he nodded.

"I thought you were doing all your interviews—dates—whatever you call them," she stammered, "here at the mansion."

"You're my last date. I'm taking you out." He held out his arm. "Shall we?"

Nervously, she put her hand around his arm. She could feel the warmth of his body through his sleeve. Feel his strength and power. Blood rushed through her veins as her heart pounded. She swallowed, lifting her gaze to his.

"Where are we going?"

Looking her over slowly in a way that made her melt inside, he glanced at her stiletto heels then gave her a low, sensual smile. "You'll see."

CHAPTER THREE

INTERVIEWING POTENTIAL BRIDES had been even less enjoyable than he'd imagined. For Omar, it had been a long day.

For the sake of the bride market, he had cleared his schedule of all diplomatic and governmental meetings today. He'd done it reluctantly, because there was never enough time for affairs of state, whether he was negotiating new trade treaties, building new business alliances or dealing with rival factions amongst his nobles.

Ruling was serious business. Unlike most billionaire bachelors, Omar didn't take holidays. He didn't *do* vacations. For fifteen years, since he'd inherited the throne, he'd been keenly aware of his duty. His people needed everything he could give. He could hardly risk their prosperity or security while he selfishly relaxed on a beach, or slept in, or went out partying at night.

He'd sworn he'd never be like his father, who'd been self-indulgent and weak, allowing Samarqara to fall into poverty and disarray and ignoring his sickly Samarqari-American wife to enjoy one mistress after another, abrogating his royal responsibilities to the powerful oligarchs, especially Hassan al-Abayyi.

But it had taken Ferida's death for Omar to realize he must never be like his grandfather, either. Yes, the man had been strong, mercilessly destroying all his enemies to maintain his grip on power, hold Samarqara together and end the civil war. But the cost of his single-minded ruthlessness had been too great. It had burned everything it touched.

A good ruler had to balance between strength and compassion. A treacherous tightrope to walk. Which was why Omar could never rest. Why he had no honorable choice but to sacrifice his own needs for those of others.

And that included marriage.

But an equal sacrifice would be demanded of his queen. Any potential bride must understand this, and realize that beneath the glitter and glamour of crowns and palaces, the royal family were, at their hearts, just servants, working to improve the lives of the Samarqari people.

The women he'd brought to Paris were all incredibly intelligent and ambitious. He'd been sure they would intuitively understand what would be expected of them.

But with a few possible exceptions—Dr. Edith Farraday, Dr. Bere Akinwande and, regrettably, Laila al-Abayyi—they hadn't. They seemed to think of Omar as a bank offering limitless investment money, or a glamorous, romantic prize to be won, rather than a potential partner in personal sacrifice.

Omar had thought the bride market would make finding a wife and queen efficient, if not easy. Simply put, he was looking for the best—a brilliant, beautiful woman with dignity, strength, integrity. A woman he could be proud to call his own, a queen who would serve the people well, a loving mother for his future children.

That was the theory, anyway.

In practice, he felt like he'd wasted an entire day, making small talk with women he couldn't remotely imagine spending a honeymoon with, let alone a lifetime.

And the one he lusted for, he could not have.

By the end of the evening, Omar had almost felt tempted to put marriage off a few more years. But even that option was lost, because thanks to the paparazzi, the whole world had now heard of his bride market. The international mockery of it was already high. If, on top of everything, it also proved a failure, leaving him still a bachelor at the end of it, both Samarqara and its king would be a laughingstock.

No. Omar had started this path. He had to finish it. In the end, if he, with the advice of his council, made the correct choice, his new queen would be admired and adored by his people. His unorthodox choice of using the bride market would no longer be a cause for mockery, but respect.

Somehow.

But first…

Omar glanced at Dr. Farraday, now sitting beside him in the backseat of the luxury SUV. His driver in the front, sitting beside the bodyguard, had managed to escape the paparazzi with skillful driving and death-defying turns down dark alleyways. Omar and Dr. Farraday—Edith—had already enjoyed a brief private, after-hours tour of the Louvre. He'd seen her beautiful face light up when she'd seen the famous *Mona Lisa*. He'd enjoyed watching her. Very much.

Now, as they drove back through the dark streets of Paris, it was very late. The privacy screen was up in the SUV, and the two of them were alone.

For better. Or for worse.

He glanced down at her, so impossibly desirable in her diaphanous silk sapphire gown that fit perfectly against her hourglass figure, lingering against her wide hips, her tiny waist, her deliciously full breasts. She was petite, feminine, perfect. He caught the scent of vanilla and strawberries in her light brown hair, falling sleekly down her shoulders, over the sensuous faux fur of her jacket.

Their thighs were just inches apart on the soft, supple leather of the car seat. His whole body was aware of her every movement. Her every breath. It was all he could do not to turn to her, push her back against the seat and crush her body with his own, plundering those sweet red lips in a hungry kiss.

Omar's body felt taut just thinking of it. He forced himself to look out at the passing lights of Paris. He knew Dr. Edith Farraday was too tactless and forthright to be his queen, if she even were willing to give up her career to be a full-time diplomat, wife and mother, which he doubted. He would not dishonor her—or himself—by betraying the laws of tradition, and giving in to his desire.

No, he'd done that once before, when he was

too young and arrogant to know better, and it had ended one life and changed others forever, including his own. Never, ever again would he try to take what he did not earn.

"Where are we going now? Back to the mansion?"

Her voice trembled. She met his gaze nervously, before her long dark lashes trembled shyly against her rosy cheeks.

He smiled. "You mentioned the Eiffel Tower."

She blinked. "You remembered?"

"How could I not?"

She looked down at her hands folded in her lap as she mumbled, "I'm not used to men paying attention."

His gaze traced the adorable smattering of freckles across her nose. "You spend too much time in the lab."

Her gaze flashed up at his in chagrin.

"Edith—"

"Beth," she whispered.

Omar frowned. "What?"

She lifted her gaze to his. "My friends call me Beth."

"Beth?"

"It's—it's a nickname."

There was something strange in her voice that

he didn't understand, especially since her eyes shone at him with honesty. More mystery, he thought, and unwillingly leaned forward in the back seat of the SUV, searching her gaze in the moonlit Paris night. "As you wish. Beth."

She looked relieved, and then a wicked gleam came into her eyes as she murmured, tilting her head, "And shall I call you Omar?"

He narrowed his eyes at the breach in protocol. As he was king, no one was ever allowed to use his first name, unless and until expressly invited. Had no one told her?

Then he saw her mischievous grin and realized she was teasing. She expected him to refuse. She was counting on it.

Humor. The one thing no other woman had tried today.

"Of course," he replied with equal innocence. "Omar."

He said that to shock her, and he succeeded. He smugly noted her wide eyes and parted lips. "I was kidding!"

"I am not."

"But, Your Highness, I couldn't possibly—"

"You will call me by my first name." He was distracted by the flick of her pink tongue against the corners of her red lips. He wanted to kiss those lips. Hungered for them. "Let me hear you say it again."

"I couldn't," Beth stammered in the silence, broken only by the hum of the SUV's engine and the traffic noise as they drove through Paris. She took a deep breath. "Look, Your Highness—"

"Omar," he corrected fiercely. The command he'd given her as a response to her joke suddenly was an absolute need. He wanted to hear his name on her sensual, delectable lips.

She licked those lips nervously.

"Omar," she whispered.

Her voice electrified his body. He went so hard, he nearly groaned aloud, just from hearing the two syllables of his given name on her mouth, on her lips and teeth and tongue and breath.

What was happening to him?

He'd never felt such attraction before. He clenched his jaw. He had to put a stop to this, regain control.

He should have his driver return to the residence. He should have his servants escort Beth to her room and put her on a plane back to America at once. Because Omar could not let himself feel this way. Not when he knew he could not choose her as his queen.

Or could he?

The thought infiltrated his soul like a whisper of wind through the wavy green grasses over the sand dunes of the southern Caspian shore.

Had he been hasty counting her out? Could Dr. Beth Farraday be his bride?

No, he told himself firmly. Lust was not enough. She would make a terrible queen. She was committed to her lab. Sacrificing her research would be out of the question. She was too outspoken. Too careless of the opinions of others. Too awkward in high society.

Too warm. Too sensual. Too joyful.

Why would a woman like that wish to be trapped in the gilded prison of a royal palace?

"I have a question," Beth said softly. She peeked at him out of the corner of her eye. "You don't have to answer if you think it's rude."

Curiosity pricked him. "Go on."

"Why are you doing this bride market stuff?" She shook her head, looking wistful. "You're good-looking, charming, rich, powerful. I mean, if someone like *you* has a hard time finding a partner, what hope is there for the rest of us?"

"I wasn't having a hard time," he corrected, stung. "I simply wished to honor my country's traditions, and be efficient in my choice of queen."

She snorted. "Efficient? You're spending millions!"

"Money means little to me. Not as much as quickly finding the right woman."

"But—why not just marry a Samarqari girl?"

Beth was probably thinking about Laila. His jaw tightened. "My grandfather did that. But when he elevated one noble Samarqari family over all the others, a quarrel turned into a civil war, which spread as all families were forced to pick sides." He set his jaw. "Half a million people died, including all my grandmother's family and nearly everyone in my own, except for my father, who was eight years old, tucked in a Swiss boarding school."

He watched as the color drained from her face. "I'm sorry. I didn't know the history."

"I'm sure." Omar allowed himself a smile. "It's something I admire about you."

She snorted. "My total ignorance?"

"Your single-minded devotion to your life's work." Looking at her, he said quietly, "My older brother died of biphenotypic acute leukemia when I was a child."

She turned pale. "I'm… I'm so sorry."

"I'm only telling you so you'll understand how much I respect what you're doing." Slowly, he reached out a hand and tucked a long tendril of her hair back from her face. "I admire you, Beth. So much."

He felt her shiver. Her eyes were wide and luminous in the moonlight.

He realized his hand was still tangled in her long hair. It felt soft, so soft. He wanted to move his fingers against her cheek. He wanted to stroke her full, swollen bottom lip with his thumbs. He wanted to kiss her deeply, and reach his hands beneath her fur coat to stroke every luscious curve of her body in the blue dress.

The SUV stopped. They'd arrived at the Eiffel Tower, overlooking the shadows and early spring greenery of the Champ de Mars. A moment later, the back door opened. His uniformed driver waited.

Omar got out of the SUV, then reached back for Beth. Just touching her hand made it difficult not to kiss her. For a moment, after the driver departed, the two of them stood on the dark, deserted sidewalk, their hands remaining entwined beneath the moonlight.

"Why have you never married before now?" she whispered.

The question made pain slice through his throat. He pushed the vicious memories away. "Because I did not wish to."

"That's no answer."

"Isn't it?" He thought of his mistresses in the past. Cool blondes with cold natures, quickly seduced, quickly forgotten.

Nothing like this. Nothing like her. A woman like Beth, so open, so direct, so obviously kind, would be a partner for life.

"You asked me why I did this, Beth," he said in a low voice. "Why did you?"

Her cheeks went pink, and she bit her full, red lower lip. She looked away. "I told you. For the money. And to see Paris."

Yes, she'd said that before. But, for some reason, this time her words bothered him.

What had he expected? That she'd suddenly confess that, busy and weighed down with the responsibility of her obligations, she'd secretly hungered for a real human connection—more than a temporary lover, a permanent partner? That she'd say she'd been disappointed too many times by romance, and had never completely gotten over a devastating tragedy of the past? That she'd say, for the sake of her country, she'd decided to cast her fate to the winds and settle for whatever the universe offered her?

No. Beth Farraday was a scientist. She didn't believe in fate. Not the way that Omar did. But growing up as he had, as the leader of his nation, he'd seen too many coincidences, split-second turns of fortune that, like a flip of a coin, could have gone either way, not to believe in fate.

Like the fate that had made him king, when his older brother had died too young.

Like the fate that had caused Omar, fifteen years before, to choose a bride who already secretly loved another man, who'd taken her own life rather than be forced to become Omar's queen.

No. That last wasn't fate. It had been Omar's fault alone, for selfishly, blindly, putting his desires above all.

Beth's eyes cut through him. "What is it?"

He'd intended to interrogate her. Instead, he had the sudden discomfiting thought that she saw right through his outward mask to the pain beneath. He dropped her hand. "Come. I've made special arrangements for our visit."

As they walked beneath the base of the Eiffel Tower, she tilted her head back, her eyes dazzled by the lights illuminating the monument as well as the Paris night.

"I've never seen anything more beautiful," she whispered.

Omar looked at her joyful expression, at the way her hazel eyes danced. "I have."

It was such a small thing, bringing her here, and yet she seemed almost intoxicated by happiness. For a smile like that, he thought, he would have taken her to a thousand Eiffel Towers.

Strange that Beth Farraday wasn't impressed by the thought of becoming a queen, a billionaire's wife, the envy of half the world. But she was overjoyed by the thought of seeing a tourist attraction visited by millions of people every year.

"It's just too bad it's closed," she sighed.

"Not for us," he said.

"What do you mean?"

With his bodyguard following at a discreet distance, he led her to the private entrance, where he spoke quietly in French to a waiting guide. It had been arranged as a favor for the King of Samarqara, in the interest of international diplomacy.

Omar turned back to her. "Stairs or elevator?"

"Stairs."

"There's a lot of them," he warned.

"I'm not scared."

He smiled, liking her fearlessness. "This way."

They walked up the stairs to the first platform, and then the second. Even in high heels, she kept up with him. When they came out onto the viewing area, she gasped. She couldn't look away from the beauty of the city at their feet. And he found he couldn't look away from her.

"Thank you," she whispered, looking out at the sparkling lights of the French capital. He saw tears in her eyes. "I'll never forget you made this possible."

"You're giving me too much credit."

"You're wrong. I'll always remember this moment," she said fervently, and he found himself wishing that she was talking about him, not some iconic building made of steel.

Was it irony, or punishment, that he hadn't had that thought about any of the other nine potential brides?

No, not nine. Eight. He'd ignored Laila al-Abayyi's existence after their brief introduction in the salon. She was the only one he'd refused to meet with privately today.

For the other eight, Omar had dutifully knocked on their doors at the residence to escort them to the garden or salon or library for a private hour of discussion. Half had giggled and blushed, as if all their obvious sense had surrendered in face of the primordial Cinderella dream. The other half spoke to him as if they were at a job interview, giving well-planned business presentations about whatever company or cause they were hoping he might invest in, while also giving him subtle signals they might be interested in taking the discussion to bed.

None of them seemed interested at all in the political and economic situation in Samarqara, and how they personally could influence the country. None bothered to interview Omar as a potential mate or lifetime partner. Did they not realize the seriousness of this choice?

No, he thought dimly. How could they?

But the last woman had truly shocked him, when she'd bluntly offered him a blow job in her bedroom to "seal the deal"—offering it with cold eyes, as if it were a simple transaction: one blow job equaled one royal crown!

Omar shuddered. Sia Lane might be the most famous movie star in the world, but she left him cold. He'd immediately refused, stating the simple truth that the tradition of the bride market did not allow him to even kiss any woman, until he'd chosen her formally as his bride.

Sia had shrugged. "Fine, follow protocol. But I'm the best. You'll choose me."

Perhaps he should, in spite of his distaste. It wouldn't be hard to convince the council to select an internationally famous movie star, who'd create huge publicity for Samarqara. And at least she wasn't Laila, the half sister of the woman whose life he'd unthinkingly destroyed.

When Omar closed his eyes, he could still imagine Ferida walking out into the desert to die.

"What are you thinking right now?"

Beth was looking at him. *Through* him. As if she saw everything, all the faults and weaknesses, which, as king, he fought so hard to hide and repress.

Of all the many reasons he couldn't choose to marry her, this was the strongest of all.

"That the night is growing cold." An icy wind blew against them on the platform, and he turned, holding out his arm. "Come. Dessert has been arranged."

As they were seated in the glamorous restaurant inside the Eiffel Tower, they were given the very best table. They were the only customers, as the restaurant had officially closed hours ago. Beth's face lit up like a child's when she saw the view, and they were served a variety of French pastries and cheeses on a silver tray.

"*Bonsoir*, mademoiselle. Monsieur." The French waiter smiled at Beth, then bowed his head respectfully to Omar in turn. "Would you like to begin with coffee or champagne?"

"Are you kidding?" she blurted out. "I drink coffee all the time. I'll have champagne!"

As they sipped a very expensive vintage, the servers discreetly disappeared. Beth looked out at the amazing view of Paris, and he looked at her in the soft glow of the flickering candle on their table. The gold-red light moved over her cheek, over the curve of her throat and sensitive corner of her bare neck. Over her collarbone, and lower, to the enticing shadows of her breasts.

"So what do you—" As she turned back to look at him, her voice abruptly cut off. He relished the pink blush that rose on her creamy cheeks. She licked her lips, and he nearly groaned. She swallowed, then said, "So…what do you think so far?"

That I want you in my bed, now, Omar thought. "About what?"

She tilted her head quizzically. "About your choice of bride. How's it going?"

It was going badly, since the woman he wanted was the one he could not have. Though his body was working overtime to convince his brain otherwise. "I must take my time to choose the final five, who will return to Samarqara to meet my council. They will choose the one they feel best suited to be Queen."

She looked horrified. "You don't make that choice yourself?"

"Yes...and no." He looked at her. "I nominally have the final say, of course. But only a fool would discard their advice. Because by the laws of Samarqara, once a child is conceived in a royal marriage, divorce is forbidden."

"No divorce—ever?" Her eyebrows lifted in consternation. "That seems really harsh. Not to mention impractical. What if you—" she hesitated "—fall out of love?"

"Since we will never have been *in* love, that is not a concern." He took a drink of champagne. "The law is for the good of the nation. Half siblings fighting for the throne caused endless wars in the last century."

"Do you have a lot of wars?"

"Not since I became king."

Her eyes went wide. She looked at him with new respect. "Wow."

His forehead furrowed. "Wow?"

"I just realized how much pressure it must be, being king. All the responsibility. Preventing wars. It's not just castles and crowns."

"No. It's deadly serious."

"Where is Samarqara, exactly?"

"It's on the southern edge of the Caspian Sea." His lips curved upwards. "On the old Silk Road, a small kingdom rich with oil and spices, famous for its ancient learning and the warmth of its people."

"Your economy is built on oil?"

"Oil and trade. Our finance industry has also grown in the last fifteen years. But we aren't a tourist destination. Not yet. Not like our beaches and fine weather deserve." He paused. "Though my tourist board estimates that if I marry Sia Lane, worldwide tourism to Samarqara would increase by five hundred percent."

Omar expected her to mock such a practical consideration, to express her horror and disgust at the thought of him marrying the movie star, horror he privately shared. But Beth just looked thoughtful as she nibbled on a sweet *baba au rhum*.

"That's a lot of new tourists."

"Yes."

She sighed. "And I can see how the happiness of your people must matter more than your own." Shaking her head, she said sadly, "In some ways, as king, you're the least free person in your entire kingdom."

Omar stared at her in the shadowy restaurant. No one had ever said such a thing to him before. Of its own accord, his hand reached for hers across the table, even as he said quietly, "It is my birthright."

"I guess, but… Who can you even talk to, when you have problems?" Beth looked down at her small hand wrapped in his. "How do you even have friends? You're the king. By definition, you have no equal." She lifted her head. Her luminous eyes went through him as she whispered, "You must feel totally alone."

A shudder went through his soul.

All the other women today had approached him strategically, like generals with a war to win, as if Omar were someone they had to conquer to achieve their deepest dreams.

But Beth wasn't trying to conquer or convince. She wasn't even weighing the consequence of her words. She had no fear. She wasn't talking to him as someone addressing a king, or even like they were on a first date. She was talking to him like he was just a person.

Like an equal.

She wasn't worried about speaking that way to a king, because she wasn't trying to get him to invest in her research—in fact, she'd totally ignored his attempts to even discuss it. And she'd already voted herself out of the running to be his bride.

Why? he thought suddenly. Because she knew he wouldn't choose her?

Or because she wouldn't choose *him*?

"Sia Lane would make a beautiful queen," she continued sadly. "She's so famous. You're right. Everyone would want to visit Samarqara." She licked her red lips, and his eyes devoured the small flick of her wet pink tongue against the corners of her mouth. "But…"

He met her eyes. "But?"

Beth looked at him. "Shouldn't your choice of bride be based on more than the recommendations of your tourist board? Your council will see that, won't they?" Her gaze fell to his mouth as she whispered, "Even though you're king, you're also a man."

Yes. A flesh-and-blood man.

Looking at Beth across the table of the elegant, empty restaurant, with the flickering shadows of a candle between them and all the sparkling lights of Paris beyond, Omar knew a hunger he'd never known before. He wanted her. Almost more than he could bear.

Gripping the edge of the table, he fought his desire with all his force of will. He wanted to sweep the silver champagne bucket away, throw the dessert plates aside in an explosion of crumbs and push Beth back against the table. All he could think about was how it would feel to have her lips hot and hard against his, her body soft and yielding, to hear her gasp with answering pleasure and desire as he pulled up her gown and took her, pumping into her hard and fast until they both exploded. His body demanded he stake his claim, possess her, with all of the lights of Paris at their feet.

But Omar was king. He could not. It wasn't just honor at stake, but common decency. Soon, within days, he would be an engaged man. He could not seduce a woman he did not intend to wed. It would dishonor them both.

He took a deep breath, then another, not allowing himself to move an inch, except for the involuntary tightening of his jaw as he looked down at her across the table.

Beth's expression changed. Her full, red lips parted. From the corner of his eye he could see the sway of her full breasts, as she took a deep breath and started to lean forward—

Turning, he rose abruptly to his feet.

"The night is late." His voice was low and harsh. "Allow me to escort you back to the mansion, Dr. Farraday."

"Yes," she said, rising unsteadily in her turn. "Of course. I've been greedy with your time."

This time, Omar did not hold out his arm for her. He could not. He was afraid that if he touched her, he might lose his razor-thin hold on his control.

As they descended in the elevator of the Eiffel Tower, they were both silent. She looked at him only once.

"Thank you, Your Highness," she whispered, her eyes full of emotion. "I'll never forget this night."

As the elevator opened, Omar knew neither would he.

Damn it to hell.

* * *

Beth's nerves were tight as the chauffeur drove them back from the Eiffel Tower to the royal residence. She was overwhelmed with guilt. She had to tell Omar the truth about her identity. She had to!

No, you don't, she could almost hear her sister arguing. The only reason the king would need to know the truth, Edith had texted her firmly, would be if he were seriously considering her as his bride. *Which is impossible, obviously*, her sister had added.

Beth agreed, even if she thought it somewhat unkind of Edith to point it out. But it was true. Beth was surrounded by nine women who were all better queen material than her. Well, eight, at least.

She was going home tomorrow. There was no way he'd choose her in the top five, not when he was so serious about finding a woman with the skills to reign a nation. Not her, obviously. So why would Beth blurt out the truth now, and tell Omar that she wasn't a world-famous cancer researcher but just a nobody? Even worse, revealing the fact that she'd been lying to his face all this time?

If she told him now, it might briefly make her

conscience feel better. But then she'd lose all the good that the two million dollars might do— curing childhood cancer!—when he demanded it back after she confessed her lie.

It was dangerous enough that she'd asked him to call her Beth. Even now, as she thought of how it had felt to hear her own real name on his sensual lips...

She shivered in the back of the SUV. Glancing at Omar out of the corner of her eye, she thought of how gorgeous he was, how devastatingly charming, how rich and powerful. It would be different if she thought he might be actually considering her as his bride. But it was obvious to everyone, Beth most definitely included, that she didn't fit into Omar's elite, sophisticated world.

No. If there was any attraction, it was on her side alone.

So she said nothing as they arrived at the mansion. Silently, he walked her through the residence, his sheikh's robes skimming the marble floor, as he escorted her to her bedroom.

"This is me," she said awkwardly when they reached her door.

"Yes." His voice was low. Electricity crackled between them as their eyes locked. His eyes held such fire that for one moment, she had the wild thought he intended to kiss her.

No. She had to be mistaken. Anyway, he'd be kissing Edith. Not her.

But it had all started to feel so jumbled. He was calling her Beth now, not Edith. His lips would be caressing hers, not Edith's.

He thought of her an amusement, nothing more, she told herself desperately. Men saw Beth as a pal, someone to confide in about the gorgeous women they actually desired. And hadn't Omar asked her to give him romantic advice about the other potential brides?

But as he took her hand, a strange zing went through her. Her hand tightened involuntarily as she felt the strength and power of his larger fingers pressed between her own. With an intake of breath, she looked up at the dark embers of his eyes. Then her gaze fell to his hard-edged jaw, laced with five o'clock shadow, and his sensual mouth.

He leaned forward, and she breathed in his scent, of sandalwood and spice.

"Beth," he said huskily, "I have a question I must ask. Even though I already know the answer."

Had he figured out she'd lied about being

Edith? Was her decision to continue lying all for naught? Her voice squeaked, "Yes?"

Omar's gaze burned through her. Her heart lifted to her throat. Then he said, "Would you ever consider giving up your career?"

Was he—could it even be remotely possible that he—?

"Yes," she blurted out without thinking. "For love."

"Love?" His expression changed. "Is that important to you?"

"What's more important than that?" she whispered, looking at him, thinking how easy, how completely easy it would be, for her to let herself fall.

"Love." His lips twisted. "I'm astonished. You'd give up your research? Your lab? Your life's work? For something as unpredictable as emotion?"

"Love is more than that—" Beth started to protest, then all the air was sucked out of her lungs as she realized she'd answered as herself, not Edith. There was no question that *Beth* would be happy to give up her minimum-wage job working in a shop, for a man she really loved, to raise their children and create a real home. What could be more meaningful than that? She cared about *people*, not work. Her job was just a job. Not a joy.

But Edith wouldn't answer that way. She'd never give up her work. Not for love. Not for anything.

"I'm sorry, I... I misunderstood," she forced herself to say. "I could never give up my work in the lab. Not for any reason. My work is my life."

He gave a single, short nod. As he dropped her hand, his shoulders looked tight. "As I thought."

There was a noise down the hall. Sia Lane, dressed in tight exercise clothes and carrying a water bottle, was coming down the hall, apparently returning to her room after a workout in the residence's private gym.

"Miss Lane," Omar greeted her politely. "Exercising? At two in the morning?"

"I believe in physical activity. At any time," the movie star purred. She glanced down at Beth in her faux fur coat and blue silk gown with a smudge of chocolate at the neckline, and sniffed, "But then, I have discipline."

Her cold blue eyes made it clear that she thought Beth was sorely lacking in that respect. After she passed by, continuing down the hall toward her room, Omar turned back to Beth.

"Well." Silence fell between them, and he said

in a low voice, "It was a pleasure to see Paris with you."

Beth's heart fell. This was the end, she knew. She told herself it was for the best. Even if she really had been Edith, it wouldn't have worked out. Edith would never have chosen marriage, not even to a king, over her job. Not in a million years.

Tomorrow, Beth would return to Houston. She'd never see Omar again, except perhaps in news stories. She'd read about his wedding to one of the other women she'd met here tonight.

She took a deep breath, fighting back tears.

Squaring her shoulders, she forced herself to smile and stuck out her hand. "You're right. I guess this is goodbye."

He took her hand. His dark eyes were unreadable. "Goodbye?"

"Good luck with your choice tomorrow." She tried to ignore the sensation of her hand in his. She lifted her chin. "It was great meeting you. I know you'll help your council make a great choice, whether it's Laila or Bere or one of the others. Whomever you choose, I hope you'll be happy together. I hope you fall in love with her."

His lips curved arrogantly. "I told you—"

"Yes, I know. You think love should be no part

of it. Just do me a favor." She lifted her gaze. "When you choose your wife, choose from your heart. Not the advice of your tourist board."

Omar looked at her, then his hand suddenly tightened on hers. "Come with me."

"With you?"

"To Samarqara. I want you there. As one of the five."

Beth nearly staggered back from shock. "You—you do?"

"Yes."

"But I'm all wrong to be your queen!"

His dark eyes were grim. "I know."

"Then why?"

He lifted her hand to his lips. "I need you."

He needed her?

Beth's whole body, her whole being, trembled from the inside out as she felt the warmth of his breath against her skin, the brief hot caress of his lips against her hand.

That was all it took—a kiss on the hand. An old-fashioned, chaste gesture. And she felt the world shake as emotion and desire whirled around her like a tornado, leaving her stunned.

"Say you'll come," he commanded.

"Yes," she whispered.

He straightened, releasing her. For a moment,

she swayed, looking up at him, still lost in the storm.

"You're an extraordinary woman, Dr. Farraday," he said huskily, cupping her cheek. Then he turned and left.

Beth watched as he disappeared down the hall. A dazed smile lifted her lips.

Then her smile dropped. If he was actually considering the possibility of making Beth his wife...

Oh, no.

Her heart twisted. It meant she had no choice now but to tell him the truth. And Edith would just have to give back the money. So be it. Beth couldn't lie to him anymore. She couldn't risk hurting him—

"So he didn't even kiss you." The voice was a sneer. Turning, she saw Sia Lane standing behind her in the hallway, still in her exercise clothes, her beautiful face incredulous.

Beth wished she would go away. "He kissed my hand..."

"Your hand?" The movie star snorted. "He's a sheikh. A billionaire king. If he's only kissing your hand, it's pretty clear what he thinks of you, isn't it?" She looked over Beth contemptuously. "And who can blame him?"

Pain filled her heart. "Why would you say…"

"I heard you're the only girl he took out to see Paris. Big deal." Coming closer, Sia whispered with vicious satisfaction, "We spent our date in my bedroom. In my bed."

Beth felt sucker punched. "I don't believe you."

She shrugged. "Believe me or not. Men always want me. You and I both know who was born to rule. And who was not." Looking Beth up and down scornfully, the movie star turned on her expensive running shoes, tilting her skinny hip. Gripping her small towel and water bottle like weapons, she said pleasantly, "See you in Samarqara."

Numbly, Beth went back to her own bedroom, closing the door behind her.

Just a moment before, she'd been half in love with him, just because he'd kissed her hand. Because he'd looked into her eyes. Because he'd made Beth feel, for one night, like she was truly extraordinary.

But she wasn't.

She heard the echo of Wyatt's voice. *I'm sorry, Beth. You're just too…ordinary.*

She heard Alfie's, when after six months of oddly chaste "dating" she'd disastrously tried to kiss him the night of senior prom, and he'd flinched away. *I'm sorry, Beth*, he'd told her mournfully. *The truth is, I've never been remotely attracted to you.*

And now this. No wonder Omar had been so late to knock on Beth's door that night—he'd been busy seducing Sia Lane. Beth sucked in her breath. All the time, while she'd been putting on lipstick, brushing her hair, imagining she might be pretty, he'd been kissing the beautiful movie star. And doing more than kiss her.

He's a sheikh. A billionaire king. If he's only kissing your hand, it's pretty clear what he thinks of you, isn't it?

Feeling sick, Beth covered her face with her hands. Of course he'd choose Sia Lane over Beth. What man wouldn't? No matter how mean and rude the woman might be, she was too beautiful and glamorous to be ignored. So Omar had slept with her. Then he'd tried to blame his preference for Sia on the tourist board.

For the love of heaven, the *tourist board*!

A choked sob came from the back of Beth's throat. How could she ever have imagined, even for a moment, that the two of them had forged a connection? That Omar might actually be considering her to be his wife?

She'd been right all along. Omar had never

seen her as a desirable woman, or potential bride. He'd seen her as a pal, just like the rest.

It was for the best, she tried to tell herself for the umpteenth time. But her throat ached with pain. Wiping her eyes, she reminded herself about the extra million they'd get for cancer research after she went to Samarqara. And seeing that Beth was only an amusement for the sheikh, not a real contender, she had no reason to feel guilty.

But that no longer made her feel better. Not this time. Not when she'd just been sucker punched by this final proof of what her heart had always known.

There was nothing special about her. Nothing at all. And there never would be.

Leaning back against the door, Beth cried.

CHAPTER FOUR

BETH DIDN'T SEE Omar at all on the flight to Samarqara the next morning. He'd already left Paris earlier, on one of his other private jets.

"The king must travel separately from us. It's required," Laila al-Abayyi, who'd also been selected as one of the five women for the bride market, told her with a smile.

"Traveling separately? Why?" Beth asked, sitting beside her in the jet's lavish cabin.

"Tradition. But it could be worse." Laila grinned. "In the old days, the king's potential brides had to arrive either by camel across the desert, or by rickety ship across the Caspian Sea!"

Beth returned a weak smile. But her heart felt sad. Even the thought of seeing exotic Samarqara didn't lighten her spirits. All she could think about was how happy she'd been last night, when Omar had kissed her hand and made her shiver, as his dark eyes pierced her soul. *I need you.*

Yeah. He needed her for advice. As a friend. Looking woodenly out the window, Beth took a deep breath. Then she thought again of how hard it must be to be king, how lonely.

Omar al-Maktoun did need a friend, she decided. Setting her hurt aside, she set her jaw. So a friend was what he'd get.

Beth would do everything she could to make sure he ended up with a bride who could actually make him happy.

She heard Sia Lane talking loudly on the other side of the plane about her latest worldwide blockbuster. The two women she was talking to, Taraji, a Silicon Valley executive, and Anna, an internationally known attorney, looked bored.

Beth wished Bere Akinwande, the Nobel Prize–winner, could have been here. But at breakfast that morning, all ten women had been presented with a contract they had to sign in order to be chosen to travel to Samarqara.

The vizier told them tersely. "He requires you each sign, before I can announce the final five."

"And if we don't sign?" Bere had asked.

"Then you won't have even the chance to be chosen," the vizier had said with a smile.

Feeling wretched and a little hung over, Beth had looked at the contract. The language was simple, asking each woman to assert that she had no impediment to marriage, and that she was interested in Omar as a potential husband—knowing that the wedding that would take place within a month, would require the bride to live permanently in Samarqara, and that if pregnancy occurred, would be indissoluble.

There were murmurs of dismay from around the table. "Of course he's gorgeous and I'd love to date him," Bere said, alarmed, "but...marry him in a month?"

"And immediately have children?" Another woman sounded horrified. "I don't care how sexy the man is, I barely know him!"

"And there'd be no escape hatch of a divorce if it doesn't work out!"

The vizier's smile widened. "If you cannot agree, then please do not sign."

Strange, Beth thought. Rather than trying to convince the women to sign, the man seemed almost pleased that so many were backing out.

But others at the table were more eager. Laila al-Abayyi signed it at once, barely bothering to read the words. The lawyer from Sydney was next, followed swiftly by Sia Lane and the Silicon Valley executive. For all their obvious success, they seemed eager to toss aside the daily grind of difficult careers for the fantasy of running away to an exotic land to live in a palace as the bride of a devastatingly handsome sheikh king.

"What about you?" someone asked Beth.

"Only four signed," someone else pointed out.

"Four is enough." The vizier scowled as he turned to Beth. "Dr. Farraday, there's no need for you to—"

Not waiting, Beth took a pen and signed *E. Farraday* with trembling fingers. Her sister's name, but hers, too—*E* for Elizabeth. She had no concern about a quick marriage or pregnancy or the lack of possibility of divorce. Because Omar wouldn't choose her.

She could still remember how she'd felt when Omar had kissed her hand. *I need you*, he'd said. *Say you'll come.* And she'd answered, *Yes.*

For the sake of that promise, she could endure twenty-four hours more. Then she'd go home to Houston with three million dollars for her brainy sister to save the world, and return to being invisible at the thrift shop—forever.

It was all Beth wanted now. All she could hope for. To return to her ordinary life, to her ordinary self, and to never, ever give any man the opportunity to hurt her like that again.

But first, she had to prevent Omar from choosing Sia as his bride. Even if he didn't realize how miserable she'd make him, Beth did. So she'd act like the friend he needed. She'd save him from himself.

Now, sitting on the plane, Beth looked at Sia still talking loudly on the other side of the cabin. She still couldn't believe Omar had slept with Sia. Every time she thought about it, she felt sick.

But she still didn't get it. "Why would Sia Lane sign that contract?" Beth said slowly. "She's a movie star with the whole world at her feet."

"Because Omar's gorgeous, and a king," Laila replied. She called him by his first name, Beth realized. Her heart twisted in spite of her best efforts. "Besides—" the girl tossed her head "—her last three movies were flops. And she's thirty-six years old. Being a movie star doesn't last forever."

"What about you?" Beth said. "Why do you want to marry him?"

Laila's expression changed. She gripped her hands together so tight that the knuckles were white. "It's my birthright."

Her words echoed Omar's. Beth wondered if the girl was already half in love with Omar, too.

They seemed perfect for each other, she thought sadly.

Pushing the pain in her heart away, Beth said brightly, "You should be queen. I'm going to say that when I dance with the king tonight."

Laila looked at her with almost tearful gratitude. "Thank you."

Lulled by the low hum of the plane, or perhaps the unshed tears stinging the backs of her eyes, Beth curled up in her white leather chair and fell asleep. She woke to find Laila gently shaking her.

"Samarqara." She pointed. "That's the capital city, Khazvin."

Looking out the porthole window, Beth was awed by the exotic beauty of the city in the warm golden afternoon light. She saw minarets and domed buildings in sapphire blue, next to squat clay houses, beside new glass-and-steel skyscrapers overlooking the sparkling Caspian Sea.

But after the jet landed it wasn't the view that hit her first. It was the warmth.

Unlike Paris, which was still held by the last gasp of winter, here in Samarqara there were flowers in bloom, and the sun shone golden in the bright blue sky. Palm trees waved lazily in the softly stirring breeze, redolent of sea and spice, as the five potential brides were taken by waiting limousines through the city to the vizier's gilded palace.

"Welcome to Samarqara," the vizier greeted them, spreading his arms wide. "You will be staying at my palace until the bride market tomorrow. Tonight, there will be a ball, so the nobles of the high council can meet you and decide who amongst you is most worthy."

The women looked at each other nervously.

"What about the king?" the Silicon Valley executive demanded boldly. The vizier gave her a thin smile.

"He will dance with each of you just once at the ball tonight. Then, after the parade of brides through the market tomorrow, he will take the advice of his council and formally announce his decision from the steps of the royal palace."

"So we're just traveling through a market? That's how the bride market got its name?" Beth said in relief. "I was afraid we'd be offered for sale, like candy bars with price tags!"

The vizier looked down his nose. "It's ceremonial, Dr. Farraday. You'll be brought from my palace on palanquins and carried in a parade through the souk—that's the old market square—before being presented formally to the king at the royal palace." He turned to the others. "Welcome to my home. You may choose how to spend the afternoon. Rest and prepare for the ball tonight, or if you prefer, tour the city."

"Rest," four women said in unison.

"Tour," said Beth.

An hour later, Beth was met by a smiling Samarqari tour guide. She spent the afternoon listening to the girl's every word, wanting to learn as much as possible about this fascinating country. She drove through the city streets of Khazvin, sampled Samarqari dishes, listened to the traditional music. She was shocked to learn details about the horrible civil war of two generations before that had wiped out a third of the population.

"And even after the war ended, our country struggled in poverty..." Then the tour guide brightened. "But since King Omar came to the throne, Samarqara has been blessed. Now we await his choice of queen and the birth of an heir, and our happiness will be secure."

Her eyes glowed. Beth blushed beneath her gaze. She clearly thought Beth might have a shot at the title.

After just a few hours looking at the sights,

they returned to the palace too soon for Beth's liking. As the driver, accompanied by a body-guard and the tour guide, drove them back through the city in the SUV, Beth noticed people stopping to stare at them from the sidewalk, peering toward the darkened glass windows.

"Why are they doing that?" Beth whispered.

"They want to see you," the tour guide replied, smiling. "They're curious about the woman who will someday rule them."

"It won't be me, I'm afraid," Beth said wistfully. She looked out at the beautiful city.

"You're too modest, Dr. Farraday. You are the best choice."

Beth turned to her with a frown. "Why do you say that?"

"Because you are the only one who cared enough to see my country," the girl said simply. "And so I shall tell all my friends. Though alas—" she sighed "—they are not on the high council."

After they arrived back at the vizier's palace, Beth lingered in the foyer.

"Please. Just let me try the words one more time."

The tour guide nervously glanced to the right

and left of the grand foyer of the palace. "Are you not in a rush to get ready for the ball?"

Beth snorted. She didn't need to impress the council. She was just Omar's buddy. His pal. She could have worn sweatpants, if that wouldn't have been an insult to both the king and his nobles. But she wanted to have good manners, as her grandma had taught her, and that meant learning the words. *"Please."*

The tour guide sighed and said doubtfully, "As you wish."

The tour guide had earlier tried to teach her a few words of the Samarqari dialect. But learning languages had never been Beth's forte. She'd managed yes—*nem*—and no—*laa*. But the phrase she really wanted to learn, the traditional greeting to respected strangers, *Peace and joy be upon your house*, had made the tour guide look alarmed every time Beth tried to say it.

Now, as Beth attempted the phrase yet again, the young woman gasped. "Honored doctor," she begged, "you must never say that phrase, ever again."

But after the guide left, Beth continued to stubbornly practice the phrase in her mind. *Peace and joy be upon your house.* How bad could her pronunciation really be?

A maid escorted her to her assigned bedroom in the vizier's palace—another truly lavish suite, with a view of slender palm trees and the blue sky over blue water. Beth was ready before she needed to be. She looked at herself in the mirror. Another night, another fancy dress. This one was the fanciest of all, an emerald ball gown, the softest whisper of silk against her skin. She brushed out her light brown hair until it gleamed and put on makeup. She looked at herself in the mirror. Her eyes were sad.

Tonight was the last night. She had to make it count.

Beth was the last to be called downstairs. She saw the other brides whispering to each other in the hall outside the ballroom. Then, one by one, the women were formally presented to the Samarqari aristocracy—including the high council.

While Beth, the Sydney attorney and the Silicon Valley executive were met with courteous, disinterested applause, half of the nobles seemed to go crazy with cheers for Laila, and the other half rooted for Sia Lane, "the most famed beauty in the world!"

Beth wondered ironically how long the nobles would clap for her after they actually got a chance to talk to her. She pushed the thought away. She was determined to have good manners, no matter what.

When Beth was introduced to the five elderly men of the high council, and their wives, she swallowed hard, lifted her chin, and spoke the traditional Samarqari greeting, the one she knew would really impress them.

"Peace and joy be upon your house," she proclaimed proudly in Samarqari.

The eyes of the old men went huge with shock. There was a tinkling crash as one of their wives dropped a champagne glass.

"Beth."

She jumped when she heard Omar's husky voice behind her. With an intake of breath, she turned. And swallowed hard.

In Paris, he'd been sexy, strong, irresistible. But in Samarqara…

Here, Omar was king. His absolute power was like a light shining from the white fabric of his robes. Everywhere he walked, his people looked at him with awe, servants and nobles alike, as if he wasn't just their king, but their greatest hope and joy.

Looking up at him now, Beth's heart squeezed so tight in her chest she almost couldn't breathe.

For a moment, in spite of all her vows to think only of finding him a good wife, all she could feel was the fervent, desperate regret that she couldn't be the woman in his arms. Instead, he'd slept with Sia. The last woman on earth who deserved him.

He looked past her, toward the shocked members of the council, then took her arm. "Dance with me."

"Now?" she stammered.

"Right now."

"But—but I was introduced last. The vizier said I'm supposed to dance with you last."

"It's my decision to make," he said grimly, and there was no arguing with that.

Nervously, Beth allowed him to lead her onto the dance floor. Music started, with a haunting melody played by exotic musical instruments. They danced together slowly, barely touching, beneath the weight of all the people watching them.

This was the last time she'd ever be in his arms.

Good, she told herself, trying not to cry. She never wanted to see him again, anyway. Her heart was in her throat as she looked up at his darkly handsome face.

"What are you doing?" he bit out.

"What do you mean?" she whispered, when what she really wanted to ask was, *How could you sleep with her?* or *How could you have ever made me think I might have a chance with you?*

Omar stared at her incredulously. "You gave the high council the traditional Samarqari greeting."

Beth brightened. "Yes. I learned it today—"

"Only you said it wrong, and insulted them with a suggestion about their mothers and a donkey."

Her cheeks colored. No wonder the tour guide had begged her not to say it. "Oh."

Omar shook his head in irritation. "So answer my question. What are you trying to do? Are you trying to *not* be chosen?"

"As if I could be!"

"What is that supposed to mean?"

"We both know I'm just here for moral support. As your buddy. Your pal!"

He looked at her incredulously. "My...pal?"

She nodded, blinking back tears. "It's fine, I totally understand. Even if I'd said the words right, the council wouldn't have wanted me. I'm a failure at everything. I only came here to keep you from making a horrible mistake!" Her skin felt clammy, her heart pounding in her chest as she pleaded, "Don't marry Sia just because you slept with her!"

"What?" Omar stopped on the dance floor. "What are you talking about?"

"You don't have to hide it," she said miserably. "Sia told me all about it. How you slept together right before our date."

His voice was low. "Sia said I slept with her?"

"I'm not jealous." Beth's throat ached at the lie as she whispered, looking up at his darkly handsome face. "I mean, it's not like...not like I thought...you and I could ever be..."

With everyone watching, he pulled her back into his arms and started dancing again. He said in a low voice, "I never touched her."

"She said you—"

He glanced down at her, his expression harsh. "Under the traditions of the bride market, I cannot touch any of you. Not until I announce my choice." Setting his jaw, he muttered, "Though I was tempted."

"Tempted by Sia."

His dark eyes flashed. "Tempted by you."

Intense emotion flooded through Beth. "You—you were?" Then she narrowed her eyes. No. She wasn't going to fall for it again. "You mean as a friend."

He snorted. "*Friend.* I nearly kissed you last night. It took all my willpower to…" Setting his jaw, he looked down at her. "If Sia lied to you, it's because she feels threatened."

He hadn't slept with Sia? Because he wanted *Beth*? No. It couldn't be true. Could it?

Her pulse was as rapid as a butterfly's wings. "Threatened—by me?"

"She sees what everyone else can see. Except you." He looked down at her. "Why can you not see how beautiful you are?"

She swallowed hard. "I'm… I'm not…"

"You are," he said harshly. His jaw tightened. "But I cannot choose you as my queen."

"No," she whispered. Obviously he couldn't choose the one who'd just insulted all his high council's mothers. The one who'd lied to his face from the moment they'd met. The one who screwed up everything.

But the realization that Omar hadn't slept with Sia—and he'd actually been considering choosing Beth as his bride—was the bitterest moment she'd ever known.

Her heart cried out in grief and regret. If only things could have been different…

But no. The relationship had been doomed from the start.

Blinking fast, Beth said, "So you aren't planning to choose Sia?"

He shuddered. "No."

"Then who?"

"Only three are left." His lips flattened. "The choices are not as—robust as I hoped. My vizier was supposed to have every woman sign the contract before you even came to Paris."

"But we only signed it today. I mean, some of us did."

"I heard." His voice was grim. His dark eyes seared hers. "So what should I do, Beth?"

This was the moment. But Beth found it surprisingly difficult. It took several seconds before she could force two words from her mouth.

"Marry Laila," she whispered before her throat closed. "She should be queen."

"No."

She looked up at him with stricken eyes. "But she's beautiful and kind and—"

"You have pushed her from the beginning."

"For your sake," Beth whispered. He didn't realize what it was costing her. She took a deep breath. "Because your wife won't just be your queen. She'll be your partner. Your lover. For the rest of your life." She lifted her pleading gaze. "Laila is the best choice—"

"Is that really what you want?" he demanded.

"Yes," she said miserably.

The music ended, and he abruptly dropped his hands. "Then I will go ask Laila to dance." He gave her a short dismissive nod. "Farewell."

"Goodbye," she replied in Samarqari. Omar looked startled, and she sucked in her breath. "Did I say that wrong, too?"

"No." Omar's hot dark gaze crushed her heart. "You said it perfectly."

And he left her.

Omar's heart was full of anger. At his vizier. At Beth. At himself.

He wanted Beth. And every fiber of his being told him that she wanted him. Why else would she have signed the contract that morning?

Yes, her language skills were abysmal and her attempt at diplomacy a disaster. His council already disliked her. But he could have dealt with all that.

The problem was her career. Her research was her life. She'd never give it up. She'd said it outright. And Samarqara needed a queen, not an invisible scientist in a lab.

But no other woman was Beth's equal. Certainly none who had made the final five.

How could his vizier have made such a ghastly mistake?

It had been one of Omar's only requirements, that every potential bride sign a contract in black and white, stating that she understood the seriousness of the bride market and chose to participate with a free heart. After what had happened in the past, Omar would never again try to take a bride whose heart was not free.

But when Omar had arrived in Samarqara that afternoon, his vizier had informed him of his mistake. Omar had been outraged.

"The contracts were supposed to come first!"

Khalid had bowed deeply. "I am so deeply sorry, sire. And ashamed by my error." He paused. "So do you wish to cancel the bride market?"

"Cancel?" he'd sputtered.

His vizier had met his eyes coolly. "Or you could choose Laila al-Abayyi. She signed. She's ready."

Laila, always Laila. Even Beth had pushed the Samarqari girl on him, when Omar had desperately hoped instead to hear her say she'd consider giving up her career to be his queen. One hint of that, and he would have forced his council to give her another chance.

Instead, he had two unacceptable choices: marry Laila, or let the bride market end in failure and see his culture turned into a laughing-stock.

Omar had stared down at Beth on the dance floor. She'd felt so warm and soft in his arms. Her beautiful face was rosy from the heat, her hazel eyes luminous with emotion. And she'd just told him to marry another woman.

Anger had ripped through him.

Setting his jaw, Omar had turned on his heel and stalked away. He walked past Sia Lane, who was bragging loudly about her films' total cumulative gross to several cornered-looking council members. He glanced briefly at Anna, the Sydney attorney, and Taraji, the Silicon Valley executive, both of whom were watching him with big eyes. But he was sure, any moment now, they'd both wake up from their Cinderella fantasy and wonder what the hell they were even doing here.

That left only one.

Fine, he thought tightly. So be it.

Omar crossed vengefully through the crowded ballroom of the vizier's palace.

Stopping in front of Laila, who was perfectly

dressed as she stood talking, with impeccable manners, to the council members, including her powerful father, Omar bowed with a flourish. The Samarqari girl's beautiful face lit up.

"Dance with me," he bit out.

"I'd be honored, Your Highness," Laila whispered, her dark lashes trembling against her cheeks.

Holding out his arm, he escorted her to the dance floor. There was an audible sigh of satisfaction across the ballroom as his nobles watched them. No one was chanting Sia Lane's name anymore.

His vizier's words suddenly floated back to him. *What if all the kingdom united, and begged you to marry Laila al-Abayyi? Then you would do it?*

Omar had never imagined it could happen. But now, seeing all his nobles watching with shining eyes as he danced with Laila, he realized the impossible had just happened. His nobles had united against having a stranger as queen—rejecting any woman who mangled their language like Beth, or who stretched the bonds of civility like Sia Lane.

He'd never thought it could happen.

But Khalid had.

"I am so glad you asked me to dance," Laila murmured, her eyes lowering modestly as they danced together. "I was starting to fear you never would."

Laila was different from her half sister, he thought. Ferida had been fragile, lost. But Laila had a flash of steel beneath her deliberately demure gaze.

Perfect for a queen, he thought. She left him cold. But if she was the best choice for Samarqara…

Omar danced with Laila, watched with delight by his newly united nobles. But against his will, all he could think about was the one woman he could not have. The unsuitable young woman with light brown hair, watching them from the corner of the ballroom with stricken hazel eyes.

This was what Beth had wanted, wasn't it?

She watched as Omar and Laila danced, smiling together. He leaned forward to whisper something in Laila's ear that made her laugh and her sultry dark eyes gleam.

And suddenly, Beth couldn't bear it.

Turning, she fled the ballroom, rushing back through the deserted palace to her lonely bedroom in the vizier's residence. Shutting the door behind her, fighting back tears, she looked out the window at the silvery moonlight frosting the palm trees. She'd never felt more alone.

Grabbing her phone from the nightstand, she dialed her sister's number in Houston.

Edith had told her she'd stay hidden at the lab while Beth was in Paris, to make sure no one would realize they'd switched places. But Edith hadn't answered any of Beth's messages since she'd left Houston.

That wasn't unusual. Edith never answered her phone. She was always too busy.

Even when their grandmother was alive, Edith hadn't come back once for Christmas at the small dusty ranch in West Texas. Beth had been the one to visit from Houston, to call their grandmother every day, and arrange her funeral after she'd died. She'd been the one to agonize over the paperwork as the bank foreclosed on the ranch. Edith had ruthlessly put her work ahead of everything and everyone.

"I'm close," her sister would always mutter. "So close to a breakthrough."

And yet the breakthrough never came.

Beth always told herself she didn't mind. Edith was a genius, and of course geniuses had to be treated differently from other people.

But now, as the phone rang and rang, for the first time, Beth felt something she'd never felt before. Angry.

All the times she'd been there for Edith—why couldn't her sister be there for her, just once, when Beth's heart was breaking, and she felt so alone?

Hanging up, Beth tossed the phone aside.

She slept badly that night, caught up in dreams. But the morning still came.

Beth was dressed in a traditional Samarqari gown, with long, brightly colored embroidered skirts, robes and headdress. Her eyes were lined with black kohl, her hands dyed with intricately patterned henna.

Following instructions, she left the vizier's palace to find five elaborately carved and painted covered palanquins waiting, in a parade led by royal Samarqari horseguards, at front and behind.

Feeling too sad to smile at the other four brides, Beth climbed awkwardly onto the pillows inside her own palanquin. It was lifted with a lurch by the four burly, uniformed carriers. She grabbed the soft mattress beneath her for balance.

The vizier came to speak to her. "You must

not open the curtains until you arrive at the royal palace," he told Beth rudely. "Be silent. Be small." Then he closed the curtains on her palanquin violently.

He didn't seem to like her much, she thought dimly. But then, could she blame him, after the way she'd insulted the council yesterday?

Beth resolved to remain quiet and invisible from now on. As they left the vizier's palace in a noisy, slow-moving parade, she resolutely tried to follow the rules, as silly as they were.

Beth stared at her closed curtains as they traveled the mile toward the royal palace on the hill. She ignored the voices calling out, pleading for the brides to look, to taste, to come and try this or that. Then she heard children, and she couldn't resist.

Peeking around her curtain, she saw small children following them eagerly. When they saw her face, they cheered. It seemed the height of bad manners not to respond to them.

Her earlier resolve forgotten, she pushed aside the curtains and slid awkwardly out of the palanquin in her elaborate gown and headdress. The carriers stopped with a gasp, holding the palanquin steady so she didn't fall on her face.

The kids came forward, cheering noisily, and

so did the other people in the souk. The palanquin carriers looked at each other nervously. Beth wondered if she was making a mistake. Ahead of her, she saw the other four palanquins, all of them with curtains closed as ordered, leaving her behind.

"Hello," Beth said in English—she didn't want to risk another international incident by mispronouncing anything—and smiled warmly. "I'm so pleased to meet you."

"What is your name, miss?" one of the children called in English.

"Beth." She leaned forward. "What's yours?"

As crowds came toward her in the crowded market square, she braced herself for questions. But they didn't ask any. They just welcomed her.

"Try my fig, mademoiselle, we have the greatest figs!" a merchant said, holding it out.

"And this," a plump woman called to her. "My honey pastry is the best in the world."

Beth tried both fig and pastry, leaving her fingertips sticky with honey. She licked it off with relish, to the crowd's delight. As someone asked for a selfie with her, Beth posed with a ready smile. And all the while, people were speaking around her, eager to tell her about their king.

"Miss Beth, if His Highness chooses you, you're blessed."

"King Omar, he has done so much for this country."

"He's sending my girls to college…"

"He saved my son's business…"

"Our country, it is the happiest place now in the world."

And they looked at her, waiting for her reaction.

"I love this place already," she told them honestly. "Any woman would be honored to be Queen of Samarqara."

They beamed at her.

Ahead of her, the other palanquins had disappeared entirely from the souk. The other brides were following the rules. None had even opened their palanquin's curtains.

She heard a loud noise behind her and turned. She gasped when she saw her stopped palanquin had blocked the path of the royal horseguards behind them. One of the soldiers, a scrawny-looking youth, seemed to be struggling to hold back his mount.

Everything happened in a rush.

A toddler, perhaps three years old, ran forward to join the clamoring older children. He didn't notice the nervous horse, a thousand pounds of muscle barely controlled by the young soldier astride him.

Beth heard a woman's terrified scream as the oblivious, smiling child rushed headlong beneath the sharp, slashing hooves—

Beth moved without thinking. She snatched the toddler out of the way, turning her body to protect him as she held up one hand in the horse's line of sight. Surprised, the animal stepped back. Desperately, she softly whispered calming words, as she'd done to the horses back at her grandmother's Texas ranch when they were hot or confused or scared.

For a split second, she saw the animal's bared teeth and hooves and thought she was about to die. Then the horse's eyes stopped rolling. The soldier regained control of the reins, and Beth exhaled, handing the toddler to his mother, who threw her arms around her child with a sob.

"Beth," someone suddenly cried in the crowd.

Within seconds, it turned into a noisy chant. "Beth! Beth! Beth!"

The palanquin bearers looked at each other uneasily.

"Queen Beth," someone shouted.

"This is who we want. Our queen!"

Beth listened with shock. These people didn't know anything about Edith or all her sister's many accomplishments.

They were shouting for Beth. Just for her.

"If you please, most high," one of the carriers bowed deeply, looking at her with new respect.

She looked back at the enormous crowd, now overflowing with people chanting her name. Her throat was dry. Uh-oh. What had she done, breaking the rules? The vizier wouldn't like this at all. And more importantly, neither would Omar...

Hastily, she climbed back into the palanquin and slammed the curtains firmly shut.

But it was too late. As the bearers lifted the weight of the palanquin to their shoulders and started to leave the crowded souk, she could still hear the crowds chanting her name.

Beth peeked out as they reached the grand steps of the royal palace, and was dismayed to see the crowd had only grown larger, following them, still shouting her name.

The palanquin stopped, and then was slowly lowered.

"Welcome," Omar's voice rang out, distant and cold.

The crowds fell silent. The ceremony had begun.

As planned, the brides all stepped out together from their palanquins, in perfect unison. Well, except for Beth, who was a single second behind, getting tangled in her dress and hot with embarrassment at the renewed chant of the crowds behind her.

"Beth! Beth!"

She felt the glowering anger of the four other women, as all five of them stood in a line beside the resting palanquins, looking up at the king standing on the palace's steps far above them.

"Beth! Beth!"

Ignoring the noise, she took a deep breath and lifted her chin. Above her, she saw Omar in full regal robes, standing at the top of the steps, surrounded by his council and honor guard.

Trying to shut out the glares of the other women and the nobles, and the death stare of the vizier, she focused only on Omar.

His handsome face was a furious scowl.

She ducked her head, her cheeks hot. Because of her actions, when he announced his chosen bride—Laila—the moment would be ruined, overshadowed by his people's demand for a different woman.

She'd spoiled Omar's ceremony, simply by not following the rules, simply by being herself.

"Beth! Beth! Beth!"

Omar lifted his hand in a single gesture, and the crowds fell into silence.

"I have chosen my bride."

His deep, husky voice carried on the wind. Beth looked around the royal square, with its palm trees and lush flowers, and burbling stone fountain beneath the blue sky.

"My new queen will be…"

Omar stopped. It was so quiet Beth could hear the plaintive call of a seagull, soaring high overhead. The pause stretched out as he looked from Laila, dignified and still, standing regally beside the first palanquin, past Sia, Anna, Taraji, to Beth at the very end.

Omar's eyes met hers, and her heart twisted. *I nearly kissed you last night*, he'd said. If things had been different, if he'd just been a regular guy she'd met at the thrift shop—

But he wasn't. And no amount of people cheering could make her Samarqara's queen. The council already despised her. How much more would they detest her if they knew Beth had been lying about her identity all this time, and was just a shop girl from Houston? And Omar… he would hate her.

He had to marry Laila. It was the best way this could end. Tears lifted to her eyes. The only way.

So why didn't he just announce Laila's name, already? *Just say it*, she thought fiercely, her whole body tense as she blinked back tears.

"I choose..." Omar took a deep breath. "Dr. Beth Farraday."

She froze, stunned, unbelieving. The crowd behind her screamed with joy.

For a shocked moment, a wave of happiness went through her, greater than she'd ever known.

Then her blood turned to ice, as she realized what she'd done.

CHAPTER FIVE

STANDING ON THE platform at the top of the palace steps, Omar heard his vizier's furious hiss. "Sire!"

Turning, Omar said flatly, "The choice is mine."

Khalid's face was dark with fury. "But the council chose Laila!"

They had. Unanimously. A situation so unusual it was no wonder, even now, that Omar heard the members of the council muttering darkly around them.

He had grimly planned to accept their advice, and announce Laila's name. Though he couldn't imagine taking any woman to his bed, or having any other woman at his side, but Beth.

Looking down from the palace steps, he saw her, and sucked in his breath.

Black kohl lined Beth's eyes, her lips were a slash of scarlet, and her hair was veiled in the traditional headdress. So different. So familiar. She looked like everything he'd ever wanted.

He'd felt a sharp pain in his throat as he opened his mouth, trying to force himself to speak a different woman's name.

Then a miracle had happened.

He heard his people shouting Beth's name. Chanting it to the rhythm of the blood rushing through his veins.

"Beth! Beth!" his people had begged.

And his heart had stopped.

Was he king, or not?

Beth was right, he suddenly realized. Whatever his council advised, he was choosing more than a queen today. He was choosing a wife. A lover.

He wanted Beth. And if the only thing that stood between them now was her career, so be it.

She could keep it.

"Dr. Beth Farraday," he'd heard himself say, and his people had gone crazy with joy.

"Why?" Khalid ground out now.

Narrowing his eyes, Omar said in a voice that would brook no opposition, "Because I want her."

His vizier's jaw tightened. "But she'll never give up her career."

"I know." Omar's voice was clipped.

Khalid's eyes widened in shock. Then he bowed, still radiating resentment.

It was no wonder Khalid was still pushing Omar to marry Laila. After all, Hassan al-Abayyi was a second father to him. Khalid had grown up in their house, after losing his parents.

But surely, Omar thought wrathfully, it would be best for Samarqara if he married a woman he actually wished to bed? A woman who would clearly be an excellent wife and mother? A woman whom his people already adored?

What more obvious sign could there be, than that in just the short time it took for Beth's palanquin to travel through the souk, she'd somehow already made them love her?

Beth stood at the bottom of the royal palace's wide steps, her eyes wide and uncertain as she looked from Omar, to the crowds cheering wildly behind her, then to the rejected brides now simmering with fury—especially Laila al-Abayyi. He could hardly blame the Samarqari girl for being upset. She must have heard of the council's decision, and expected her patience would be rewarded today.

But they could never suit. She'd eventually realize that.

Omar saw Beth whisper something to her

nearest palanquin bearer, and the man whisper back, nodding his head toward the palace steps.

Beth took a deep breath. Holding up the edge of her elaborate Samarqari gown so the hem didn't get dirty, she started to climb the stone steps toward him.

When their eyes locked, all of his senses heightened. He heard birds singing in the blue skies, and smelled sweet roses and the soft, salty wind off the Caspian Sea.

When Beth reached the platform, she looked pale and scared. He saw her sway, and reached out and grabbed her arm. Trembling, she looked up at him, her eyes huge.

And he did what he'd longed to do from the moment he'd first seen her in the dark cool shadows of the Paris garden, wearing a too-tight dress as she'd artlessly informed him that no sensible woman would ever wish to be his bride.

Now, pulling her roughly into his arms, Omar lowered his head to hers and claimed her with a hard, hungry kiss.

He felt her intake of breath, felt her shake. But he held her fast, kissing her deeply, crushing her smaller body against his own. Her hands, raised to push against his chest, surrendered and instead wrapped around his shoulders. To the delight of the crowd, she kissed him back, slowly at first, then with a passion that matched his own.

He barely heard the crowd's deafening cheers. With Beth in his arms, he forgot his vizier, his nobles, the other women.

He felt only this. Her.

It was as if Beth were the first woman he'd held in his arms, the first he'd ever kissed. He felt like an untried virgin, kissing her. Excitement electrified his body, turning sinew and muscle and bone to molten honey. He felt dizzy with need. He leaned her back to deepen the embrace, overwhelmed by the ravenous hunger that consumed him—

"Sire," his vizier hissed, and Omar again heard the shouts of the crowds, and remembered he was holding the future queen in his arms.

Straightening, he pulled away from the kiss. But his heart was still racing as he looked down at her.

Beth's eyes were wide and her cheeks pink. She sagged against him, as if her legs were weak.

"Omar," she whispered. "There's something I should…" Glancing out of the corner of her eye at the council around them, then at the huge crowd in the square, she bit her lower lip. With a shuddering breath, she choked out, "We need to talk."

His eyes, which had fallen to her deliciously red mouth, swollen from his kiss, rose to meet hers. "Talk?"

"You don't—" She swallowed, then said in a low voice for him alone, "You don't know who I am."

"You're Dr. Beth Farraday. Brilliant, a prodigy, one of the most famous research scientists in the world. And the woman I want to marry."

She'd looked scared before. Now she looked sick. "I'm not…" She glanced at the nobles, who'd come forward to listen. "Not worthy of you."

Not worthy? He marveled at her modesty. "Are you worried about your career?" he said quietly. "We'll figure it out. You can move your lab here."

She didn't smile. "My lab."

"Who knows." He gave her an encouraging smile. "As queen, you might lead an explosion of scientific and technological advancement in Samarqara." His smile lifted into a grin. "Even the tourist board will be thrilled."

But she wouldn't smile back.

Was it possible she didn't want to marry him after all?

No, Omar couldn't believe that. She'd signed the contract. And after the way she'd just kissed him—

She wanted him. He'd stake his life on it.

For nearly a thousand years, Omar's ancestors had ruled this land. He was the last heir. The al-Maktoun line was threatening to die out completely.

But now, as Omar looked at his bride-to-be, he suddenly knew he'd made the right choice. Because he could imagine no outcome that did not involve him getting her pregnant repeatedly. Perhaps they'd have five children. He looked over her face and body hungrily. Ten?

He wanted her so badly he didn't know how he'd manage to wait to bed her until after the royal wedding ceremony, scheduled a month away.

All he wanted to do was get her alone, rip off her headdress and elaborate gown. He wanted them both naked with their bodies entwined. He wanted to push deeply inside her, again and again, until her softly sensual body was rosy and flushed as she screamed her pleasure, digging her fingernails into his skin…

With a shuddering breath, Omar looked at her. His hand tightened on hers, then he held it up high, turning to face the crowd. "In one month's time," he cried loudly, "we will have a royal wedding, and she will be crowned your queen!"

This time, the cheers were so loud the stone thundered beneath his feet. With a final wave, he turned and escorted Beth past the columns, inside the pointed arch that led into the royal palace.

Her hand was unresponsive in his own. As Khalid and his council followed, Omar led her through the grand rooms of the royal palace. But she walked as if hardly aware of their surroundings.

"What happens to the other four?" she whispered. Trust Beth to worry about their feelings, he thought.

He shrugged. "They'll be escorted to the vizier's palace, where their bags have already been packed. They'll leave Samarqara within an hour." He paused. "Except Laila. She may stay. She's, after all, a citizen."

Beth looked relieved. "Good."

He frowned. "You don't need to worry about them. They'll return to their extremely successful lives with three extra million dollars, a new wardrobe and an interesting memory."

Beth seemed strangely intent. "But Laila—"

Omar stopped, putting his hands on her shoulders. "Forget her. I want to talk about you. About us."

He felt her tremble beneath his hands. Then she took a deep breath, glancing back at the glowering advisors and sour-faced vizier.

Following her gaze, Omar said, "Thank you for arranging the bride market, Khalid. It succeeded beyond my wildest dreams." Looking at Beth, he took her hand in his own. "Your service will not be forgotten."

"Sire," the vizier said in a pinched, unhappy voice, "if we could just talk, for a brief moment…"

Looking down into Beth's luminous hazel eyes, Omar's only thought was how to get his bride-to-be alone. He growled, "Later."

"But, sire—"

"Later." He turned to the men coldly. "That will be all."

His advisers bowed and scattered beneath his glare. Only Khalid lingered, his long face tight with repressed anger, before he, too, bowed and disappeared down the wide palace hallway.

"I don't think he likes me," Beth said.

"Khalid is stubborn, but he will soon realize what a treasure you are." He paused, tilting his head. "How did you make the people chant your name?"

A shadow crossed over Beth's eyes. "It was my fault. I knew I wasn't supposed to stop the palanquin, but I couldn't resist…"

As she relayed the story of how she'd saved the child from being trampled in the market square, Omar stared down at her in wonder.

He wondered how he could have ever considered any other woman but Dr. Beth Farraday, even for a moment. With deep respect, he lifted her hands to his lips, and slowly kissed her knuckles, one by one, allowing the warmth of his breath and lips to linger against her skin.

He felt her shiver. Then she blurted out, "Omar—I have to—"

Three maids walked down the hall, passing them with wide eyes. Omar's hands tightened on hers. "Let's go somewhere we can be alone."

Swallowing hard, Beth said in a stilted voice, "Yes."

Tugging gently on her arm, he led her down the hallways of the royal palace, past the elaborate pointed arches and columns, beneath tiled ceilings soaring high overhead in colorful patterns of lapis lazuli and gold leaf. Omar was proud of offering Beth such a beautiful home.

He'd overseen the palace's restoration ten years before, determined to make it even better than it had been, before it had been destroyed by war in his grandfather's time and neglect in his father's.

He led her up past the lavishly restored throne room, the ballroom, the salons. He barely paused to point out a two-story library filled with books, including parchment and scrolls thousands of years old, from the time of the caliphs, containing the history of his country that he couldn't wait to share with her.

Later.

Finally, he led her up the sweeping stairs in the tower to his bedroom. "This is the king's bedchamber."

Beth gasped, looking at the high ceilings, the patterned stucco of the walls. "It's beautiful."

"The most beautiful room in the palace. Except for the queen's."

"Separate bedrooms?"

"Tradition," he said huskily. He cupped her cheek. "There's a connecting door."

But as he lowered his head towards hers, she abruptly pulled away, looking as if she were about to cry. Turning, she walked out onto the balcony.

The air blew in fresh from the sea, making

the white translucent curtains undulate in the soft spring breeze. Beth gripped the edges of the balcony, looking out at the sparkling water with haunted eyes.

Omar came up behind her, putting his hands against the balcony railing around her. Directly below the tower were the palace gardens, with trimmed hedges and palm trees, and a profusion of roses in bloom. To the right and left of the palace, he could see the prosperous city, stretching out in old buildings of squat clay beside steel skyscrapers.

"I always see you with flowers," he said huskily. "Like where we first met."

She glanced back at him. "In the garden in Paris."

"I noticed you at once."

She gave a low, rueful laugh. "Because I was stupid. I was the only person who didn't recognize you."

"You spoke to me as an equal," he said. "Not seeing me as a prize to be won."

"My equal?" Beth shook her head sadly. "No. Not at all." A small smile traced her lips. "But I tried to forgive you. I told myself it wasn't your fault you were good-looking."

He gave a low laugh. "Then imagine how I felt when I met you."

She blushed in confusion. "What do you mean?"

Omar looked down at Beth, dressed in the traditional headdress and gown of a Samarqari bride. Electricity pulsed through his body. All he wanted to do was kiss slowly down the length of her naked body. He was hard and aching to claim her as his own. But their wedding was still a month away.

Omar whispered, "You were the sexiest woman I'd ever seen."

Beth looked at him sharply, as if she thought he were mocking her. Then her eyes widened.

Glancing back at his bedchamber, he gave her a crooked grin. "This tower used to be the king's harem."

She snorted. "Harem?"

"The palace is hundreds of years old. It's been built and rebuilt, from the time caravans traveled the old Silk Road. But harems were outlawed a hundred years ago."

"Too bad," Beth said, flashing him a teasing grin. "You could have saved yourself a lot of trouble by just bringing all twenty women here directly."

He returned her grin, then his expression changed.

"But I only wanted one." Pulling her into his arms, he looked down at her, cupping her face with his hands. He whispered, "I only wanted you..."

And he lowered his mouth to hers.

He felt her shock, felt her hesitation when he kissed her.

Then he felt her body rise. Her small arms reached up to his shoulders, and she kissed him back with answering need, as the salty sea breeze whirled around them.

Breaking off the kiss, he whispered against her lips, "I want you, Beth. Now."

He heard her intake of breath, and felt her tremble as she gripped his shoulders desperately, holding him close.

It was all the permission he needed. Lifting her into his arms, he carried her back into the bedchamber, to the enormous royal bed upon which no woman had ever slept. Omar had never brought a mistress here. This bed wasn't meant for any temporary lover, quickly discarded.

He'd decided long ago it would only be shared with his wife. His queen. It was the bed upon which they'd conceive their children. He'd saved it only for her, as a sign of respect.

Setting Beth down on her feet beside the bed, Omar gently tugged off her elaborate headdress. In the light from the windows, her light brown hair shone gold as it tumbled down her shoulders.

Walking around her, he slowly undid the ties that held together her traditional Samarqari gown, allowing that, too, to fall in a *whoosh* to the priceless rug on the cool marble floor.

Beth stood before him in only a simple, traditional cotton shift. His body stirred, and he knelt at her feet, pulling off her shoes. But as he rose to take her in his arms, she stopped him with an intake of breath.

"I can't. We..." She swallowed. "We can't."

Omar drew back.

"Why?" His jaw tightened as he said harshly, "You do not want me?"

She shook her head with a low laugh filled with desperate regret. "You know I do." She looked at her feet. "I never imagined you might choose me, in spite of everything. If I had..."

His heartbeat had recovered from the sickening lurch, and he came closer. "If you had?"

"I never would have come to Samarqara. I..."

She took a deep breath, then whispered in a voice almost too low for him to hear, "I'm not who you think I am."

"Why do you persist in thinking so little of yourself?" he said incredulously.

"I'm not being modest." This time, her laugh was bitter. "You think I'm some world-famous genius."

"No."

She looked up at him. "No?"

"You're more," he said quietly. "You're the woman who made my people love you in the space of an hour. The woman who risked her life to save a child. A woman who wants the best for everyone, except perhaps herself." Reaching out, he ran his hand softly through her hair. "The woman who will be my wife, and the mother of my children."

She shivered, her lovely face stricken as she lifted her gaze to his. "How can I even tell you?"

What could be troubling her? Then, looking down at her, Omar suddenly knew.

Gently, he took her hands in his own. "If you're worried because you're not a virgin, Beth, don't be." He snorted. "That's one old custom no one expects. Me least of all."

Her jaw dropped. "What?"

"You're sexually experienced. That's fine. So am I. It doesn't make you unworthy. It doesn't make me want you less." Cupping her cheek, he said in a low voice, "It only makes me want you more."

That was a lie, Omar thought. Nothing in this moment could make him want her more.

Her eyes looked shocked. She looked quickly away.

"Isn't that what you wanted to tell me?" he asked, confused.

She shook her head, her expression anguished. She clasped her hands, twisting them together.

"I…the thing is, I'm not…" She focused on him abruptly. "I'm actually a virgin." Her gaze fell to his lips. "So I couldn't possibly please you in bed, anyway."

Shocked, he stared at her, hardly able to believe her words. "You're a—virgin?"

"Yes. Another reason I can't marry you." Tears filled her eyes. "So call the other women back. Tell Laila you changed your mind. It's not too late to make a better choice!"

As he stared down at her, all he could hear were her words echoing in his brain. *I'm a virgin.*

Unthinkable. In this modern world, his bride

would be coming to his bed a maiden? Untouched by any other man?

"How is it possible?" he breathed, searching her face. "Are all the men of Houston such fools?"

Her cheeks burned red. "I've only had two boyfriends in my whole life. The first was in high school. I didn't understand why he never tried to kiss me, until at graduation he announced he was gay. And my second boyfriend..." She looked away. "I had a mad crush on him, but he was never really that into me, I guess. He broke up with me last year because...he said there was nothing special about me. I was too boring, he said. Too *ordinary.*"

Her voice was husky with unshed tears.

"Ordinary?" Staring down at her, Omar felt a flood of emotion. He said hoarsely, "That's the last thing you are."

Beth looked at him, blinking fast, as if afraid to believe his words. Taking her into his arms, he felt her body tremble against his.

Then he realized that he was the one trembling.

He'd been wrong when he'd thought nothing could make him want her more.

She was a virgin. *A virgin.*

"But I have something more to tell you." Her voice dropped to a whisper. "Something I...wish I didn't have to say."

Somewhere in the back of Omar's mind came the thought that, now he knew she was a virgin, he had no choice but to wait for marriage before he could bed her. That was the only honorable path. That was the way of the old days.

But how could he wait?

"You have to understand how expensive cancer research is," she was saying. "And how desperate my sister was." She shook her head, running her hand over her forehead. "No, that's not fair to blame her. I also wanted to see Paris."

Omar was bewildered. What did Beth's sister have to do with anything?

He didn't want to talk about their families, or the past. What did anyone else matter, except the two of them, now? Their life was just beginning...

"Later," he said huskily. He lowered his head to kiss her. His caress was gentle at first. But as he tasted the sweet softness of her lips, his need intensified. His grip on her tightened as he plundered her mouth, teasing her tongue with his own, until she abruptly ripped away.

"Please," she cried, her eyes wild. "*Please. You don't understand. I'm not who you think!*"

Omar couldn't understand. How could such an accomplished woman judge herself so harshly for what could only be some tiny, unimportant flaw?

But he saw in the wildness of her eyes that whatever it was, she was torturing herself over it.

"So tell me," he said huskily. "I want to know every bit of you. Or better yet," he whispered, lowering his head for another kiss, "show me..."

As they kissed, he thought he tasted the salt of her tears. Whatever her imaginary flaw was, he had to show her it didn't matter. He reached around her, loosening the ties of her shift, and the thin fabric fell to the antique rug beneath their feet. Beth stood naked before him, except for white lace panties.

His breath stopped as, still fully dressed in his regal sheikh's robes, he looked down at her full, naked breasts, tiny waist and long hair tumbling down over her creamy virgin skin. Her light brown hair seemed a multitude of colors, tangled strawberry and gold and chestnut. Her big hazel eyes were a swirl of blue sea, green fields, brown earth. The whole world.

He could almost hear the pounding of her heart. Hear the soft pant of her breath as she stood utterly still, her pink nipples tight with arousal. As she looked up at him, her eyes pulled him with their desperate, innocent desire. She was everything in this moment.

Need pounded through Omar so great he knew he could not wait for their wedding next month, any more than a starving man could stand beside a feast without reaching for the food that might save him. Resist? Impossible.

He had to have her. Now.

But Beth was a virgin. Only a selfish bastard would violate that, just weeks before they would wed. Her innocence was a precious, unexpected gift. He had to respect that—and her.

So he'd marry her, Omar thought suddenly. Right now.

CHAPTER SIX

WHAT WAS SHE DOING? Standing here in front of him so brazenly, nearly naked? Did she have no shame? Had she lost her mind?

Yes. Beth had. Her lips were swollen from his kisses. Her body was aching with longing. She wanted more. She wanted—him.

But she had to put a stop to this. Now. Before the impact of her deception became even worse, and he couldn't undo the choice he'd made.

She'd tried to force herself to tell him, to explain. Why was it so hard? All she had to do was say five simple words. *I'm not Dr. Edith Farraday.*

Or six: *I've been lying to your face.*

That shouldn't be hard, should it?

But it was. As Omar stood in front of her in the dappled sunlight of the lavish suite, his dark eyes burned through her. Then they traced slowly, appreciatively, down her body.

She took a deep breath, gripping her hands at

her sides. And the words that would end everything caught in her throat.

For the first time, Beth felt what it was truly like to be desired. And by such a man as this…!

Never taking his eyes off her, Omar removed his head covering. His dark hair beneath was rumpled, so soft and wild that she ached to run her fingers through it. Eyes locked with hers, he slowly removed his sheikh's robes.

Standing before her in just loosely fitting trousers, Omar looked down at her. With an intake of breath, Beth stared at the shadows and curves of his tanned, hard-muscled chest, laced with dark hair. He was so powerful, so strong, his shoulders so broad and wide. He made her feel delicate, feminine. He made her feel like the heart of his whole world.

Coming forward, he cupped her cheek and whispered, "I want you, *habibi*."

"*Habibi?*"

"It means…beloved."

Outside, the palm trees waved against the soft warm wind, dappling the golden light from the windows. Beth froze, trembling with longing she'd never felt before.

Just one night, she thought. One night to know what it was to be desired. One night to cherish for the rest of her life. Then, in the morning, she could confess everything, before any real damage was done. She'd make Edith return all the money. They'd quietly cancel the wedding.

One night in his arms, and then Beth would set him free to choose a different woman to marry. One who was worthy to be his wife, and Samarqara's queen.

The temptation of it was almost unbearable.

Beth licked her dry lips. "This is wrong," she whispered, over the pounding of her heart.

"I know."

Her eyes lifted to his in shock. "You do?"

"You are a virgin," Omar said grimly. Powerful and so masculine, he moved toward her with grace, in spite of his strength and size. "You kept faith with the old traditions. You deserve to be treated as the precious treasure you are."

Her? A precious treasure?

Unwillingly, Beth's eyes traced over the hard muscles of his chest and arms, down the length of his chest, along the arrow of dark hair that led to his taut belly, disappearing beneath the waistband of his loose trousers.

"To make love to you before marriage would be dishonorable. I know this." Cradling her head in his hands, he looked at her hungrily. "But there is only one thing that matters more."

Beth couldn't look away. No one had ever looked at her like he was right now, as if she were Christmas morning and birthday cake and the first sunshine of spring, all at once. "What?"

His dark eyes burned through her. "Do you want me, Beth?"

Did she *want* him?

No man had ever made her feel like this. And she suddenly knew no man ever would again.

Did she want him?

Already, in the short time she'd known him, she'd ridden the greatest roller coaster of her life—joy and anguish and fear and desire.

Did she want him.

Of course she did. But she couldn't have him. She didn't deserve him. If she'd been Edith—

It wasn't fair, her heart cried out. She and Edith were identical, and yet they weren't. Edith had everything, all the beauty and talent, leaving her with nothing.

Couldn't Beth at least have this? Couldn't she feel Omar's arms around her, just for one short, blissful moment? Couldn't she have something, just for herself, a moment she could always remember, before she went back to her ordinary life forever?

"I…" Tears burned the backs of her eyes as she trembled on the edge of the abyss. "I can't."

"You can't what?"

"Want you," she whispered. But as his expression fell, she couldn't bear it. "But I do," she choked out, searching his gaze. "I want you more than anything."

Omar's larger hands tightened on hers. The expression in his dark eyes pierced her heart.

"Beth," he whispered, then spoke words in Samarqari, kissing her on one cheek, then the other.

"What did you say?"

"If you truly want me, *habibi*, then say my name, and those same words back to me."

Lost in his dark eyes, in the sensation of his hands wrapped around her own, and her trembling guilt for what she was about to do, she stumbled through the words. He was so close to her. When she swayed forward, her bare, aching nipples brushed against the dark hair of his hard-muscled chest. Dizzy with longing, she breathed his name.

His handsome face glowed in the shadowy

bedroom, as the soft warm wind curled past the translucent curtains, cooling their heated skin.

"Now kiss me, Beth," he said huskily, his dark eyes burning through her soul. "My right cheek, then my left."

It seemed strangely ceremonial, but all she wanted was to keep this moment, to wrap it up so tight she'd remember it forever. Whatever it took. Whatever it cost. Her heart was brimming with emotion as she stood on tiptoes and kissed his cheek, then the other. As her lips grazed his skin, she felt its roughness, the dark sandpaper bristles.

When she pulled away, Omar's dark eyes were shining.

He lowered his head and kissed her lips, so gently, so tenderly, that her heart nearly broke inside her.

Still kissing her, he slowly pushed her back against the bed, kicking off his shoes, covering her nearly-naked body with his own. She felt his weight, his strength. She gloried in the feel of him against her, a sensation she'd never felt before.

His lips were heaven, hard and soft, as his tongue teased her, tempting her, swirling against her own. His hands moved from her cheeks, to her shoulders, where her hair spilled in tumbled waves against the pillows.

"You've made me so happy," he whispered, kissing down her throat. She closed her eyes, lost in pleasure as he cupped her full, aching breasts. She held her breath as he lowered his head to taste a taut nipple. He held each heavy breast like a tantalizing sweet to be licked and sucked into his hot, silky mouth. Sensual pleasure swirled around her, drawing her deeper, as a sweet ache coiled low and tight in her belly.

Moving up, he kissed her lips, caressing her body like the precious treasure he'd called her. He kissed her cheeks, her forehead, her eyelids. He ran his hands through her hair and back down her body. He kissed in the valley between her breasts, with a slow lick at each nipple, suckling her before moving downward, ever downward. Slowly pushing her legs apart, he knelt between them on the bed.

The roughness of his cheek scraped softly against the sensitive skin of her belly. She felt the heat of his breath, and then the flick of his wet tongue against the hollow of her belly button. A shiver went through her, but he paused for only a moment, then continued his exploration downward. Exploration?

Seduction.

As he pulled the whisper of white silk lace panties slowly down her thighs, she squeezed her eyes shut, shivering. She felt the bright, hot sun from the open window heating her naked skin. She felt the mattress sway beneath her as he removed his trousers, then knelt between her thighs. His powerful, muscular legs were bare and warm and rough against her skin.

"Beth," he commanded. "Look at me."

She obeyed, and, seeing him above her, kneeling between her thighs, she gasped. His body was tanned, hard and powerful with muscle, so much bigger than her own. And hardest of all...

She looked at his large shaft, standing erect from his body, jutting toward her. She'd never seen a naked man before. She held her breath, lost in equal parts fascination and fear.

Wonderingly, she reached out to take him in her hands. He jolted beneath her innocent touch. He was soft as velvet, hard as steel. She stroked him softly, exploring the full length of him.

He gasped. With a low growl, he grabbed her wrists, pushing them back against the pillow. He kissed her hungrily. Leaning forward, he whispered hoarsely in her ear, "Keep your hands back. Or I'll have to tie you down."

He kissed slowly down the length of her body, finally lowering his head between her thighs. She shivered as she felt the heat of his breath against the most secret places of her body. Then, spreading her wide with his hands, he lowered his head and tasted between her legs with the full rough width of his tongue.

The pleasure was so shocking, she gasped. Inexperienced as she was, she started to reach for him. But remembering his earlier words, she stopped, and forced herself to hold still, beneath the almost unbearable onslaught of forbidden joy.

His tongue moved delicately at first, then lapped her wide. As she started to tense and shake, his rhythm changed. The tip of his tongue twirled against her taut, wet core as he put a fingertip inside her, then another, stretching her.

Her head tilted back, her lips parting in a silent gasp as he worked her with his mouth. She gripped his shoulders with her nails as her hips slowly rose from the bed of their own accord. Her breasts felt heavy, her whole body tight as she started shaking all over. She held her breath. Tighter, tighter. She wanted—oh, God, she wanted—

Then she exploded, and cried out with joy, joy

she'd never even imagined existed in the world, as waves of ecstasy shimmered around her.

In that split second, she felt him move, reaching for something in the nightstand beside the bed. Then he paused.

"I've never been with a virgin before." His voice was strained. "I don't want to hurt you."

Beth opened her eyes.

"You won't," she breathed, looking up at him above her, almost dizzy with pleasure.

Positioning himself between her legs, he hesitated. Then, with a deep breath, he pushed inside her, inch by inch.

The pleasure evaporated, replaced by pain. She gasped. But as her lips parted and she started to tell him to stop, he gripped her shoulders.

"Wait," he said huskily. "Wait, *habibi*."

He'd pushed all the way inside her. He now held himself utterly still, giving her time to accept his size. And she realized the throb of sharp pain was disappearing.

As her shoulders relaxed, the grip of his hands loosened. Kissing her gently, he ran his hands down her body, cupping her breasts, biting her lower lip.

And slowly, very slowly, he began to move inside her.

Incredibly, new pleasure started to build, a new sweet tension coiling inside her, deeper than the first. Holding her breath, she twisted her head against the pillow, hair tangling around her. She closed her eyes, lost in sensation.

"No," he whispered, tilting her chin. "Look at me. Feel me as I'm inside you."

Their eyes locked, their souls joined, as he filled her, inch by inch, until she thought she couldn't take any more, then somehow, he made her take more, stretching her deeper still. Pulling back, he thrust again inside her, slowly at first, then faster as he began to ride her.

Harder. Deeper. He pushed her to the limit, thrusting inside her until, to her amazement, she exploded once again, this time, into ecstasy so deep, the whole universe seemed to burst into stars.

From the moment Omar had kissed her, it had been all he could do not to explode.

But she was a virgin. He'd had to go slow. He'd kissed her softly, feeling her naked body shiver as she wrapped her arms around him. As he'd lowered her against their marital bed, he felt the whisper of warm wind against his skin, and the heat of her body against his own. He'd felt the power of her innocent desire for him, and he gloried in it.

He'd desperately held himself back. It had been torture. He'd kissed her soft, sensual body, with her full breasts and curvaceous backside. He'd licked and caressed every inch of her, making her ready.

Then she'd suddenly reached out to touch him, wrapping his shaft in her sensual hands. He'd nearly exploded right then and there. Hence his threat to tie her down. But how else could he keep enough control over his rampaging body, when all he wanted to do was make it good for her?

Forcing himself to go slow had been the greatest feat of his life. Pushing her thighs apart, he'd stretched her wide and tasted the sweetness between her legs, teasing and lapping her with his tongue until he felt her tighten and gasp and explode. Then, with her scream of ecstasy still ringing in his ears, he'd reached for a condom.

Going slow had been torture.

It had been a different kind of agony when he'd taken her virginity. He'd hated hurting her. Holding himself utterly still, in all her exquisitely tight heat, had been almost unbearable. When her pain had abated, and he slowly began to move, he'd still had to keep a tight rein on himself. Making her explode with pleasure once wasn't enough. He'd wanted to bring her to even higher ecstasy. He'd wanted their joy to bind them even closer, as their eyes locked and souls met, as he was buried so deep inside her—

But the moment he felt her shake as she cried out a second time, her body tightening convulsively around him, he lost the last shreds of his control.

Control? He lost his mind.

Her magnificent breasts swayed as he thrust harder and faster, and then he'd exploded, racked with pleasure so intense he almost passed out.

He collapsed over her with a groan, exhausted. Their hot, sweaty bodies remained entwined together across their marriage bed. Then his eyes went wide as he saw the condom had broken.

A chill filled him, even as he tried to tell himself it didn't matter. They were married now. They wanted children.

And yet—

It doesn't matter, he told himself harshly. Tenderly, he kissed her forehead, then pulled her small, naked body protectively against his.

He must have slept, because when he opened his eyes, the shadows across the bedroom had moved, to the slant of late afternoon. His stomach growled. He considered calling for food, then glanced at the clock above the marble fireplace. The lavish dinner banquet, set to celebrate the conclusion of the bride market, was set to begin in a few hours. Perhaps it was better to wait. Especially since he did not want it widely known that he'd already seduced Beth and claimed her secretly as his bride, a month before the formal ceremony.

Though if she were already pregnant, everyone would be able to do the math...

He looked again at Beth, sleeping in his arms, so soft and warm, and a hunger stirred in him of a different sort. But as he was reaching to wake her, he heard a hard knock on the bedchamber door. He looked up in fury. Who would dare—

The door burst open, revealing his vizier and two guards.

Seeing Omar and Beth naked in bed, Khalid went pale. "What have you done?"

"What have I done?" Omar growled. Beth, blinking awake, looked horrified at having their private moment invaded. He wanted to strangle the vizier with his bare hands. As she covered herself with a sheet, Omar rose to his feet in full, naked fury.

"What is the meaning of this?" he thundered.

"That woman is a fraud, sire!" His vizier's voice lifted a trembling finger to point at Beth. "She's not Dr. Edith Farraday. The real Dr. Farraday is still in Houston, hiding in her lab!"

Omar glared at him. "What are you talking about?" He pointed toward the bed. "She's right here!"

"That's her identical twin, Beth Farraday!"

Identical twin? Omar snorted, shaking his head. "You can't expect me to believe—"

Then, turning, he saw Beth's face. The stricken expression in her eyes.

"I was going to tell you," she whispered.

And Omar's heart went numb. His body changed in a second from warmth and joy to pure ice.

He would have been prepared to fight anything, to defend the woman he'd chosen. But he couldn't fight the look on her face. It almost brought him to his knees.

Staring at her, he staggered back a step. "You... you're not Dr. Farraday?"

Mutely, she shook her head.

"Who are you?"

"I'm nobody," she whispered.

"She works in a charity shop!" his vizier said with malicious triumph.

Omar felt a shot of pain in his throat. Turning on Khalid, he said in an expressionless voice, "Leave us."

The vizier's eyes flamed with impatience. "Sire, I do not think it wise to leave you alone with this *temptress*—"

"Do not make me say it twice."

The guards bowed and obeyed. The vizier grudgingly followed, closing the door behind him with one last venomous look at Beth.

Omar stood naked beside the bed, alone with the woman whose virginity he'd just taken so gloriously as his own.

He felt like he'd just been punched.

The corners of his lips twisted coldly. "At least I know why you asked me to call you Beth."

Looking up at him, she choked out, "I'm sorry."

Sorry. His hands tightened at his sides. *Sorry.* He looked at the bed he'd saved just for his wife. For his queen. Thought of what he'd just done. Because he'd trusted her.

But she'd been lying to him all the while. Lying to his face. Destroying everything he'd tried to achieve.

Fury built inside him, choking him, freezing him from the inside out, as he whispered, "Damn you."

CHAPTER SEVEN

How had this all gone so horribly wrong? Omar was looking down at her as if she were a stranger.

"Please," Beth choked out, "you can't think—"

"Can't think what? That you lied to my face from the moment we met?" His black eyes were hard. "That while I stupidly trusted you, and chose you as my bride, you and your twin sister were laughing yourselves sick at your deception?"

"I wasn't!" Her voice shook. "We had a good reason!"

"Tell me," he cut her off.

Beth held the sheet up higher over her naked body, all the way to her neck. She took a deep breath.

"When Edith—my sister—got your invitation," she said haltingly, "she couldn't leave the lab, you see, but she really needed money for cancer research. So she asked me to come in her place."

Omar stared at her, his eyes cold.

"It was just supposed to be fun," she said weakly. "A chance to see Paris and do some good in the world."

"Do some good," he repeated incredulously.

Beth's cheeks went hot as shame filled her.

"I'm so sorry," she whispered. "If I'd had any idea you might actually choose me—I swear to you, I never would have agreed to come!"

"But you did agree," he said flatly. "You agreed to come to Paris and pretend to be Dr. Edith Farraday. You agreed to be in my top ten. You agreed to sign my contract. You agreed to come to Samarqara in my top five and you allowed me to introduce you to the world, to my country, as my bride!"

Silence fell in the darkening shadows of the king's bedroom.

Grief and regret stifled her. She hung her head, staring at the priceless rug on the floor.

"I'm sorry," she repeated numbly.

Omar turned away. He pulled on some clothes from a wardrobe. Casual ones, simple shirt and trousers.

"Please." Fighting back tears, Beth took a deep breath. "If you'd only try to understand—"

"I do understand." Omar didn't look at her.

"You made a fool of me and everything I believe in for the sake of three million dollars."

"For cancer research! Money to help my sister save lives—children—"

"I don't care what it was for." His jaw tightened as he looked out at the open balcony. Outside, the afternoon sun sparkled across the Caspian Sea. There were distant sounds of people calling across the gardens, and the noise of the city beyond the palace.

"You made my people love you," he said in a low voice. "And I hate you for that most of all."

She started to speak, then fell silent. What could she say?

He turned back toward the bed. With his face shadowed against the sunlight, she could no longer see his expression, and for that she was glad. All she could see was the outline of his body, the body that had given her such pleasure. She whispered, "I was going to tell you everything."

"When?"

"Tomorrow."

His dark eyes flashed. "Liar."

"It's true." She looked down at her body, still covered only with a sheet. For the first time in her life, she'd been selfish, and let herself experience the pleasure of his touch. But she was paying for it now, body and soul. "I made a deal with myself. One night with you. Then I'd confess everything."

"Confessing only when it's too late," he said harshly.

She frowned. What did he mean, *too late*?

"Cancer is bad," he mimicked her voice mockingly, then shook his head, clawing back his hair. "I was a fool to think any scientist would say that. Or not immediately explain every detail of your research if you thought you could get more funding!"

Her cheeks burned. She looked away, a lump in her throat. "I should have told you the truth. The first time you asked me to stay, in Paris."

"You never should have come to Paris at all." He stepped toward her, his hands tightening at his sides. "But one thing I don't understand. Why did you let me make love to you? What were you hoping to achieve?"

"I…"

"Were you trying to make me care? To forgive you?"

Looking at him, she blurted out, "No one has ever looked at me like you did. I wanted…a memory. Something I could cherish for the rest of my life, long after you'd chosen someone better to be your bride."

He stared at her, then set his jaw. "Do you even realize what you've done?"

"I'm sorry." Her voice was thick with tears. How many times could she say it? "I'll leave quietly. Just tell your people the truth, that I lied. Your vizier was right. I'm nobody. I pretended to be my sister. She's the genius. I barely finished high school." She wiped her eyes. "I'll take the first plane home and…and I'll make Edith give you the money back." She tried to keep her voice light. "You can marry Laila—"

Omar cut her off with a low, bitter laugh. "It's too late for that."

"Why?"

"We had sex," he said grimly.

As if Beth couldn't still feel that, in every sweet ache of her body! As if she didn't feel that with every wistful beat of her heart! She lifted her chin. "So?"

"You might be pregnant."

That possibility hadn't occurred to her. She sucked in her breath. "But you stopped—I assumed you were reaching for a condom—"

"I did. But it broke."

"Broke?" she repeated numbly.

"I told myself it didn't matter," he said sardonically. "Why should I worry about preventing pregnancy, making love to my own wife?"

A shocked silence fell in the bedroom.

"What?"

"That's right," Omar said in a low voice. "I couldn't wait to make love to you, Beth. But you were a virgin. I couldn't make love to you. Not honorably. Not until we were wed."

Rising horror filled her.

"Those words we spoke," she whispered.

"Yes," he said quietly. "We spoke the vows, followed by the two kisses. In my culture, it is a binding commitment."

"To my sister—"

"I didn't speak the words to her. I spoke them to you."

Beth stared at him in disbelief. They were married? *Married?* She swallowed hard, trying to even comprehend it. "But I didn't know!"

His dark eyebrows lowered like a storm cloud. "And you think that negates the words, after you've already agreed to be my bride in front of all the world? When you've signed a contract stating that you were here seeking marriage?

When you told me, in every way possible, that you were mine?"

"But I never meant—" But at his murderous expression, she took a deep breath. "Fine. So I spoke the vows. No one knows but us. We could just pretend it never happened!"

His eyes were hard. "You might be good at pretending, Beth Farraday. But I am not. I am bound by honor to speak the truth, both as a man and as a king. I do not speak lies." He turned away. "My marriage isn't just a whim. It's about the future of my nation. I chose you over Laila because I thought you could help unify my people. While you were just thinking of fun trips and raising cash—" his voice was tight "—your reckless lie could start a new civil war."

Horror went through her. She gulped.

"So what do we do?"

His jaw was tense as he looked at her. "If you are pregnant, I can never divorce you. It is the law in Samarqara. A king cannot divorce the mother of his heir. Not for any reason."

Beth looked up with an intake of breath. She could actually remain his wife? In spite of the way she'd lied? For a moment, her soul thrilled.

Then she heard the flatness of his voice.

He thought she'd trapped him into marriage. Selfishly. Stupidly. For money.

Her shoulders sagged as she sat on the bed, still naked, covered with a sheet.

"You can divorce me if you want to," she said in a small voice. "I mean, you should. I deserve it."

Omar looked down at her, saying nothing, as the shadows of the room deepened in the late afternoon.

She looked up at him pleadingly, blinking back tears. "Please. Forgive me. I'll do anything."

"Yes," he said slowly. Stepping closer, he looked down at her without touching her. She had the vision of his dark face, his burning eyes. "You will."

Omar abruptly went to the bedroom door. He looked out at the two guards.

"Make sure Miss Farraday does not leave the tower until the banquet." He looked at the vizier, hovering like a ghoul in the hallway. "We have much to discuss."

"Yes, sire." Standing in the doorway, the vizier looked back furiously at Beth, still shivering on the bed. "If I had my way, Miss Farraday, you'd be thrown into prison for the rest of your life."

Her stomach turned to ice. Prison?

"Enough." Omar turned to her. His voice was cold. "Your clothes are in the queen's chambers. The royal engagement banquet is in three hours. Be ready."

"But, Omar," she choked out. "You can't still want me to—"

He left without another word, closing the door behind him.

Alone, Beth stumbled up from bed. Grabbing her formal gown and headdress off the floor, she rushed through the adjoining door to the queen's bedchamber and dropped them on the bed. Going to the walk-in closet, she grabbed the first clothing she saw, a silk robe. Tying the belt, she paced the sumptuous suite, feeling like a prisoner in spite of the lavish surroundings.

If I had my way, Miss Farraday, you'd be thrown into prison for the rest of your life.

Omar might be furious, but he wouldn't throw her into prison.

Would he?

Heart pounding, she went out to the balcony. As the sun lowered to the west, she looked down at the sea and palace gardens. A long, hard drop.

No escape there, unless she truly wanted to end it all.

When she thought of the look in Omar's eyes, when he'd discovered her deception... A razor blade lifted to her throat. They were married now. For all she knew she could be pregnant.

There was a quiet knock at the door. Going back inside to answer it, she saw a young girl, perhaps seventeen, dressed in the modest garb of a palace maid. Coming into the queen's bedchamber, the girl bowed respectfully. "I'm Rayah, Your Highness. The king sent me to serve you."

Beth looked at the floor. "You don't want to serve someone like me."

"I begged to be your maid, Your Highness."

She looked up. "Why would you do that?"

"The little boy you saved in the market." Her face glowed. "He's my brother."

Beth stared at her, then a lump loosened in her throat. "Thank you, Rayah."

"Such a beautiful dress," the girl sighed when she saw the traditional Samarqari gown. She carefully hung it up on the door of the walk-in closet. "Now. What do you require first? Some food? A rose-water bath to prepare for the banquet?"

Food was the last thing on Beth's mind. Suddenly, all she wanted was privacy, so she could call her sister. She thought of her handbag, tucked into the closet. "Um…a bath? A bath would be great."

With a bow, the maid departed to the enormous en suite bathroom.

Rushing to walk-in closet, Beth found her phone. She gasped when she saw she'd had ten— *ten!*—missed calls from Edith. Her sister, who never called anyone, had apparently been trying to reach her for the last hour. Glancing towards the bathroom, where she heard the water running, Beth closed the closet door for privacy and dialed her sister's number.

For the first time ever, Edith answered her phone on the first ring.

"What's going on?" her sister cried. "Why haven't you called me back?"

At another time, Beth might have found Edith's question ironic, after her own hundreds of unanswered phone calls. But now, Beth's eyes filled with tears. It was good to hear her sister's voice.

"The king picked me as his bride. Can you believe it?" Her voice choked on a sob. "He announced our betrothal in front of everyone."

"I know," Edith said.

"You—you know?"

"It's all over the news. The lab phone started ringing off the hook. I saw the video of him choosing you in front of his palace. Oh, Bethie, how could you do it? How could you make him love you?"

"Love me?" Beth gasped. Bitterly, she wiped her eyes. "He doesn't love me!"

"Why else would he choose you?"

She thought of the way his handsome face had glowed when he'd spoken her name from the palace steps. The fire in his eyes as he'd kissed her.

"It doesn't matter now," she said soddenly. "He's just found out I'm not you. And now he hates me."

"Come home," Edith said immediately.

"I can't."

"Of course you can. Grab a taxi and head for the airport."

"You have to give back all his money. Please, Edith, you must—"

"Fine."

"Fine?" Beth said in shock.

Her sister paused. "This has all been more trouble than I imagined. I've been sleeping at the lab, like you asked. I've sworn my assistants to secrecy but a colleague saw me this morning."

"Omar's vizier just found out you're in Houston."

"Then it's just a matter of time before the press gets wind of the twin-switch story. Come home."

"I can't. The king's put guards at my door." Beth gave a forced laugh. "I might go to prison."

"Prison?" Edith, always so cool and controlled, gave a curse that made Beth blush. "Forget that. I'm going to send the army and the Marines and even the Scouts to get you out."

What might be an idle threat with some people might really happen with Edith, she thought. Her sister knew people. Powerful ones. "No."

"Are you sure?"

"Yes." Beth couldn't hurt Omar with a diplomatic incident on top of everything else. He clearly wanted to keep this quiet. He'd put guards at her door. Immigration would probably arrest her if she tried to flee the country—which they would be well under their rights to do, considering she'd traveled here under her sister's borrowed passport.

Beth was the villain here. No wonder Omar no longer trusted her. To all evidence, she was a cold, venal, money-grubbing liar, while he'd been honest from the start about his desire to find a suitable bride. He'd even made her sign a contract, stating that she knew what she was getting into. That she was seeking marriage. And that she was Dr. Edith Farraday.

Then she'd slept with him under false pretenses. No wonder he hated her. She deserved it.

"Beth—I'm going to get you out—"

"*No.* I mean it, Edie," Beth choked out. Gripping the phone, she wiped her eyes. "I'm the one who caused this mess—"

"Both of us caused it!"

But Edith hadn't been the one who'd chosen to stay, time and time again. She hadn't been the one who'd slept with him. "I can't just disappear. That would look like I abandoned him at the altar. I don't want to hurt him. Not more than I already have."

"Then what can I do?" her sister said anxiously. "Come and marry him in your place?"

A wrench went through Beth's heart. Her sister was only trying to help. And yet...

Edith? Marry Omar in her place?

A knee-jerk reaction came from deep in her soul. "No."

"Whew. For a second I thought you might say yes!"

"Don't worry." Beth took a steadying breath. "I'll think of something."

Could she?

For much of her life, she'd been the one everyone felt sorry for. Poor Beth, with no talents or skills, overlooked, ordinary, always failing at everything. Poor Beth.

But she didn't need help. She just needed strength. She could do this. Alone.

She'd remain here and be humble and endure, and pray she wasn't pregnant, so Omar wouldn't be trapped into permanent marriage with her.

A strange thing to pray for, when Beth had always dreamed of having a child of her own. Especially strange, because she would have given anything to be Omar's wife forever.

But not like this. Not when he hated her.

For his sake, she would pray she could set him free.

Edith sounded doubtful. "I still think I should…" There was a pause, and Beth suddenly heard muffled noises on the other end of the line, then her sister gasped into the phone, "There are two men outside my lab, demanding I come with them. By orders of the King of Samarqara!"

Beth's blood froze. "What?"

"Get out of here!" her sister yelled to them in

Houston, on the other side of the world. "Don't touch me!"

And then, to Beth's terror, the line went dead.

Omar looked up at the soaring ceilings above the small council chamber. The airy, open space was filled with light. Outside, two birds were singing by the windows. Happy. Free.

"I told you the bride market was a mistake, sire." Omar heard a note of satisfaction in the vizier's voice. He turned to him at the table.

"Your second mistake," he said coldly. "You were supposed to vet the candidates."

Khalid looked pained. "She signed the contract E. Farraday," he protested. "There are few photos of her sister. I believed she'd just gained weight."

Gained weight in all the right places, Omar thought. He remembered the sweet feel of Beth's soft body against his. He'd been so sure he'd found the woman to spend his life with. So sure that he'd immediately married her and taken their wedding night.

Khalid was right. The bride market had been a mistake.

"I don't understand why the banquet is still set to continue, sire. Why have you not thrown her from the palace in disgrace?"

When Omar had told him that he'd married Beth in the old, intimate ceremony, his vizier's howls had been loud. Now he replied, "You know why."

"Yes." The vizier's lip curled. "But why not divorce the American shop girl in private, as you married her? Announce Laila as your queen. The people's hearts will be glad when they see a Samarqari bride, and they will soon forget the other."

Omar rose to his feet, slamming the table with his fist. "When will you understand? I will not marry Laila. She still reminds me of…"

His old friend went pale. "Of Ferida."

Silence fell. Omar looked away, his heart tight.

I belong to another, for as long as I have breath.

He remembered Ferida's tortured note, written right before the desert consumed her.

I can never belong to you, even if you're the king, even if it's the law.

Omar shuddered with pain. After Ferida's death, he'd changed the law so that any woman had the right to refuse to marry, even if her parents ordered it, even if the demand came from the king himself. But he'd never wanted to risk another unwilling bride.

That was what this bride market was supposed to prevent. Instead, it had fallen apart. Because of Beth Farraday's lies.

It was just supposed to be fun. A chance to see Paris and do some good in the world.

He remembered how she'd felt beneath him in bed, the first time he'd pushed into her. How he'd shuddered with the difficulty of self-control, so desperate he'd been to please her. He'd even married her instantly, rather than disrespect her.

And all the while she'd been lying about the most basic thing imaginable: her identity.

Omar had wanted a woman he could respect and trust. Instead, he'd gotten the opposite.

Setting his jaw, Omar looked out the window toward the tall tower, where he'd left her.

I'm sorry, she'd repeated in a small, quivering voice. Had she really expected his forgiveness? he wondered bitterly. When, for the sake of money and a free trip to Paris, she'd carelessly destroyed everything he'd sought to achieve as king?

In spite of his precautions, Omar knew it was just a matter of time before the rest of the world discovered he'd been tricked by the wrong sister. His people would think him either a weakling or a fool. Perhaps they'd decide to get rid of the monarchy altogether, leading the kingdom into chaos.

From the day he'd taken the throne, Omar had tried to bring his people together, and build the prosperity of all. It hadn't been easy. As a boy he'd once dreamed of freedom, of being able to do whatever he wanted, without the chafing bonds of duty. But since the death of his older brother, that had remained just a dream.

Having a solid marriage, a partnership of friendship and trust, was his biggest dream of all. His own parents had hated each other; after his brother died, they'd separated in fact, if not name.

Omar had thought he could do better. Because how could a man unify a country, if he couldn't even unify his own home?

Remembering how happy he'd felt with Beth in his arms, he felt sick. At any point since she'd arrived in Paris—when she was chosen for the top ten, when she made the top five, when she arrived in Samarqara—she could have confessed the truth. Instead, she'd made the choice, again and again, to lie.

And if she was pregnant…

He would permanently have a liar in his bed. As his wife. As the mother raising his children, and the future ruler of his beloved kingdom.

Assuming there even was a kingdom, after it was discovered Omar had defied the unanimous advice of the high council, and rejected the most honored heiress in the land, to marry not a world-famous scientist, but a lying gold digger from Houston.

Hassan al-Abayyi would likely lead the revolt. Fairly or not, the man held a grudge against Omar for the death of his eldest daughter. He would never forgive this second insult.

Omar felt heartsick. He'd been a fool to ever let his heart and body make the choice. He should have let his brain decide whom he would marry, all along.

"Your Highness!"

Looking up, Omar saw one of the palace maids, Rayah, standing in the doorway of the council chamber. He motioned her forward. "What is it?"

"It's your betrothed, sire," the girl said. "She begs you to come to her in the tower. She says it's a matter of life and death!"

So it had already come to this. Omar's eyes

narrowed. He'd thought Beth would wait before she tried to manipulate him again. She truly must think her power over him had no bounds.

Tonight, he would show her the error of that belief.

Beth shook with anxiety, pacing back and forth across the queen's bedchamber. She'd already tried twice to get past the guards, to no avail. When she'd shrieked at them about her sister and waved the phone in their faces, they'd simply taken the phone from her. Finally, in desperation, she'd sent Rayah to the king.

"Why did you summon me?" Omar demanded coldly behind her, and in spite of everything, her heart raced as she whirled to face him.

"What have you done to my sister?"

He didn't even pretend not to understand. "What was necessary."

"If you've touched a hair of her head—"

"You think I would hurt her?" Omar stalked forward in his sheikh's robes, his expression dark. He'd showered and changed, and looked handsome and powerful. As if the events of the day hadn't affected him at all.

She held her ground, glaring at him. "I was talking to her when your thugs grabbed her!"

He held up her phone. "Who else have you called?"

"No one—who cares about the stupid phone?" she nearly shrieked. "What have you done with my sister?"

"She's taking a long vacation."

Beth sucked in her breath. "*A long vacation? Is that a euphemism?*" She gripped her hands into fists. "Like swimming with the fishes or pushing up daisies? You *bastard*—"

"Calm yourself." He looked down at her coldly. "A vacation means a vacation. She'll spend a few weeks on my private island in the Caribbean, drinking piña coladas and sunning herself on the beach."

Beth blinked, dropping her fists. "What?"

"Until we know if you're pregnant, you will continue to play the part of Dr. Farraday. Which means the ruse cannot be discovered, as it surely would have been, had she remained longer in the lab. It's a miracle it wasn't discovered before now."

That was certainly true. Biting her lip, she said suspiciously, "Are you telling the truth?"

"I'm not the liar between us." Narrowing his eyes, he held up her phone. "Can I trust you with this?"

"Who would I call?"

"A newspaper outlet, to sell your story? The American embassy, to claim you're being held against your will?"

"It's not a claim, it's a fact!"

His dark eyes burned through her. "Can I trust you to help me undo the damage you've done—to my country? To me?"

Beth hesitated, then said in a small voice, "I want to. But how?"

Omar looked down at her, his eyes cold. "The banquet begins in an hour, and you are not ready. Rayah said she filled a bath for you. Why are you not in it?"

"Seriously?" She lifted her chin. "Your nobles hate me. Your vizier wants to throw me in prison. There's no way me going to the stupid banquet will help anything. I'm not going!"

"You are."

"Forget it—"

Mercilessly, he pulled her into the gleaming marble bathroom. Outside, twilight had fallen. The shadowy room was lit with flickering candles.

"What's this?" she said, bewildered as she looked around the bathroom, set for beauty and romance.

"Rayah must have done it. I didn't," he said grimly. "Now get in the tub."

Her lips parted. "I'm not taking off my robe in front of you!"

"Get in the bathtub, Beth."

She saw by the gleam in his eyes he wouldn't rest until she was in the bath, one way or the other. Dropping her silk robe she stood before him naked in the candlelight.

His dark eyes flickered as he slowly looked over her naked body, pink in the steamy bathroom. Her cheeks burned, but she lifted her chin defiantly.

He abruptly turned away, his jaw tight. "I will leave you to get ready." His voice was almost strangled. "Come down for the banquet within the hour."

"Why is it so important to you?" Beth was holding back tears. "What can we gain from me pretending to be your future bride?"

"Pretending?" he ground out, still not looking at her. "We are already wed, even if no one knows it. The banquet is in your honor. You will respect my people, and your position, by showing up."

His words made her heart hurt. Turning away,

she climbed into the hot bubble bath, laced with rose petals. After all the drama of the day, her whole body ached with exhaustion. She leaned back in the hot, fragrant water, giving a soft groan of unwilling, unexpected pleasure.

Hearing a gasp, she looked up. Omar was staring down at her in the candlelight, his dark eyes wild.

Her breasts had risen above the surface of the water. Her skin was pink with heat, her nipples red, surrounded by bubbles and floating rose petals.

Even as she willed her body not to react, her nipples pebbled beneath his glance, every inch of her body suddenly shivering with desire.

No! She could not let herself want him! Not now! Humiliated, she moved the angle of her body so her breasts swiftly disappeared beneath the water.

His eyes found hers. Electricity pulsed between them.

"I never meant to hurt you," she whispered.

"Hurt me?" His jaw clenched, and he turned away. "No. I am merely—disappointed. You made my people love you with your lies. Now, you will make their love for you evaporate."

"How?"

"Be rude. Be unkind. Be a vicious, filthy liar." His lips twisted sardonically. "It shouldn't be too hard."

The big jerk! She swallowed back a retort. "And if I turn out to be pregnant? How can I remain as your wife if I've made everyone hate me?"

"In that unfortunate event, you can easily win back their love. I am the last of my line. If you are pregnant with Samarqara's heir, you will instantly be the most adored person in the land." He gave a cold smile. "By everyone, of course, but me."

"Oh." A lump rose in Beth's throat. He called the prospect of her pregnancy *unfortunate*. Making it clear that any child born of their union would be an unwanted and regrettable burden, forcing Omar to remain yoked to Beth, when he despised her.

And this after he'd been so determined to make love to her, that he'd lured her into unknowingly speaking wedding vows! "What about my job in Houston? I can't stay here for weeks until— until we know. I'll be fired!"

"Fired?" he snorted. "As if you ever intended to go back to work at a charity shop after you collected your three million!"

"That money wasn't for me, I told you!"

"You told me a lot of things. Why would I believe any of it?"

Beth's jaw tightened. She'd tried to apologize. To make things right. What more could she do? "Look, I've already said it's all my fault. I'm trying to fix things. But I'm getting sick of your insults. There's only so much more I'm going to take!"

Omar's eyes narrowed, but as he turned to reply, his gaze fell again to her body, her full breasts peeking above the rose petals and bubbles. Setting his jaw, he looked away.

"In that case," he said tightly, "it's best that we see each other as little as possible until the day you're escorted from my country. May fate grant that the happy day arrives soon!"

He left in a whirl of robes. She thought of a retort too late.

"Mister, I'm counting down the days!" she yelled.

But he was already gone, leaving her alone in the candlelight, her throat choked with unshed tears. Her fury melted away, leaving her shivering with heartbreak in the rapidly cooling bath.

CHAPTER EIGHT

FORTY-FIVE MINUTES LATER, as her maid helped her into yet another beautiful new gown, Beth told herself she felt nothing. Not heartbreak. Because she couldn't love Omar. And she definitely, definitely didn't feel desire. He'd treated her badly and refused to even consider her side. She would never, *never* want Omar again.

A good thing, too, since all she now had ahead of her was the painful task of pretending to be his fiancée, and waiting for Omar to get the all-clear to kick her out of Samarqara, and out of his life.

The thought made her ache inside.

"Is something wrong, Your Highness?" Rayah asked, drawing back anxiously. "Would you prefer a different gown?"

Beth tried to smooth her face into a smile. "No, it's fine. Everything's perfect."

Once dressed, she went down the steps from

the tower with a heavy heart, her heavy jeweled earrings swaying in her ears.

When she arrived at the palace's great hall, she was greeted with a coolly polite bow by Omar. Looking at her as if she were a stranger, he introduced her to a crowd of aristocrats as his future queen. They looked no more pleased than Beth at the prospect.

He held out his arm to escort her up to their private table on the dais, in full view of the nobles' tables below. She nervously placed her hand on his arm. Even through his sleeve, she could feel the heat of his skin, the power of his body.

I feel nothing, she repeated to herself desperately. But her body still trembled from the intensity and passion of his possession, just hours before, when he'd ruthlessly taken her virginity and made her world explode with joy.

Now, Omar barely looked at her. As he sat beside her at the table, his hard, handsome face was a polite mask as they listened to speeches, both in Samarqari and in English, welcoming Beth—whom they still called "Edith"—as his future bride.

Beth ate and drank by rote, hardly aware of the taste. She kept her eyes mostly on the floor, and tried to be as invisible as possible. She felt miserable.

She just had to hold on for a few weeks, she told herself, and make everyone hate her. How hard could that be? As soon as she got proof she wasn't pregnant, she could return to her old life in Houston.

Now, Omar lowered his head and whispered angrily, "What do you think you're doing?"

Beth looked at him in surprise. "What?"

"You look like you're facing execution," he said through gritted teeth. "Stop it."

"You expect me to look happy when I'm not?"

"So now, *now* you insist on total honesty?" Omar's black eyes shot sparks. "You've already proven how adept a liar you can be. So yes. Lie. Look happy. Now."

Beth tried. But at every moment, she felt aware of him sitting beside her, and anger and regret churned like acid through her soul. She wished she'd never gone to Paris—wished she'd never even heard the name Omar al-Maktoun!

During one particularly long speech in Samar-qari by an older, pompous man, Beth felt Omar's knee briefly brush against hers beneath the table. Nearly jumping in her skin, she moved hastily away. Her eyes fell on Laila al-Abayyi sitting at one of the front tables. She looked utterly comfortable in her traditional Samarqari clothing, dazzling and glamorous.

The vizier, sitting beside Laila, leaned in to whisper to the Samarqari girl. Beth frowned. Something about their body language just seemed—wrong.

As the older man's long speech finally ended, he returned to sit beside Laila and the vizier. The three of them looked sideways toward the king, and for some reason, the way they looked at him made her shiver.

"Beth." Omar's voice was terse. She scowled back at him.

"What now?"

"You're still not smiling."

"How about this?" Irritated, she stretched her face into an uncomfortable rictus of a smile.

He shuddered. "Stop."

"I can't smile, I can't frown—what do you want from me?"

"At least look pleasant."

"Like you?" she countered.

Omar deliberately smoothed his handsome features into a neutral expression that did, indeed, look very pleasant. She was irritated and a little envious that he could hide his feelings so well.

"It's not fair," she grumbled. "You've been trained."

"Trained my whole life," he agreed grimly, reaching for a jewel-encrusted gold goblet. Drinking deeply, he set it down, smiling for the benefit of the banquet tables beneath the dais. "It's how I can sit beside you, pretending to be happy about my choice."

"Do you want me to just leave Samarqara?"

"Leave?" He snorted, glancing at her coldly. "Not before you make everyone despise you as much as I do."

"These people already despise me."

"The nobles might. But not everyone. Not the servants. Not the regular people of the square."

Beth thought of Rayah, and how happy the girl had been to serve her. "You expect me to be rude to them for no reason?"

"I expect you to do whatever it takes, as long as it shows no dishonor to my country or my throne, until I can satisfyingly renounce and discard you."

"What do you have in mind?" she ground out. "Should I rip off my dress and dance naked on the banquet tables?"

His pleasant expression disappeared. "Perhaps later."

Her lips parted in shock. "I was joking."

His black eyes cut through her. "You seemed eager enough to be naked before."

Against her will, her gaze fell to his cruel, sensual lips. Her own mouth tingled. With a shiver, she turned away.

"That was before," she whispered.

"Before I discovered the truth about you."

"No," she said. "Before I discovered the truth about you."

"Which is?"

Beth met his gaze. "That you're a heartless bastard who will never forgive."

"Forgive betrayal?" Smiling for the benefit of the crowd, he took a drink from the golden goblet. "No."

This icy, ruthless king was nothing like the hot-blooded, seductive man who'd taken her virginity—the man who'd lured her with soft lips and soft words.

Blinking fast, Beth said in despair, "What happened to the man I met in Paris?"

"What happened to Dr. Edith Farraday?" was the cool rejoinder.

The rest of the banquet passed in a blur, as she

ate food she didn't taste and listened to speeches she didn't want to hear, all about Dr. Edith Farraday's many accomplishments and the glory she would bring to Samarqara as queen.

Beth looked down at her hands clasped in her lap, wishing the torture would end. Because for the rest of the banquet, during all the interminable courses and speeches, she felt Omar's every movement beside her. She felt his every breath. She still felt him inside her. And most of all, she remembered the adoring gleam in his dark eyes when he'd held her, so briefly, to his heart.

All gone. All over. So she forced herself to smile through the pain. Because even though he was her husband, he'd never truly been hers.

Glancing at her face, Omar rose abruptly to his feet.

"My friends, we thank you for your congratulations. Now, my future bride and I must take our leave. She has had a tiring day, and we have much to discuss for our upcoming wedding."

With a slight bow, Omar took her hand, helping her from the table. She pasted a frozen smile on her lips as they departed the hall, hand in hand.

But the moment they were alone, she yanked her arm from his grasp. Or at least, she tried.

"You don't need to escort me back to my bedroom."

"Wrong," he said grimly, holding her fast. "How else do I know you won't try to run away?"

"I won't!"

"We've already established I can't trust you." His hand was tight as he pulled her up the twisting stairs of the tower. He hesitated at his own bedroom door, then took her to the queen's chamber. Once inside the elegant bedroom suite, Omar shut the door behind them. His eyes were grim as he faced her.

"Fine," Beth said, wrenching her arm away, desperate for him to leave before she fell apart. She yanked the elaborate headdress off her head. "I'm safely in my room. Now you can go!"

He watched as her hair tumbled down her shoulders.

"Yes," he muttered. "I will."

But he did not move.

Trembling beneath his gaze, Beth leaned her hand against the cool stone wall for support. "Please," she whispered. "Go. Now."

"Yes," he whispered, even as he drew close to her in the shadowy room, lit with dappled moonlight from the open windows. She could smell the faint scent of salt from the sea, exotic jasmine and spices. "I'll go."

He was so close to her. She licked her lips, and he groaned.

"Beth," Omar said hoarsely, "you're killing me—"

And he swept her into his powerful arms, pushing her against the wall as he lowered his mouth to hers in a rough, hard kiss.

Omar had wanted to humiliate Beth. To make her pay.

All night, he'd been simmering. She'd lied to him. She'd made a fool of him—and his country's traditions. And for that, he'd never forgive her. For that, he'd intended to make her pay.

But it seemed hating her wasn't enough. Because he was already doing the one thing he'd sworn to never do again. Kiss her.

With a low curse, he abruptly let her go.

"Why did you do that?" Her big hazel eyes were agonized, filled with both pain and desire. The same way he felt right now.

Everything about Beth in this moment, from her elaborate Samarqari gown to the firm posture of her shoulders, made her look like a queen. He would have been proud to have her as his bride, if she hadn't lied. If things had been different—

Closing his eyes, he turned away.

He took a deep breath, then said in a low voice, "I should not have kissed you."

"No." Her voice was heartbreakingly quiet.

Setting his jaw, he took three steps toward the adjoining door to his own bedroom, then tightened his fists and turned to face her. "This is intolerable. Starting tomorrow, you will do your best to make my people hate you. Until they are begging for me to take someone else as my queen."

"So you said. But how can I be rude?"

He allowed himself a grim smile. "Look at what Laila al-Abayyi does. And do the opposite."

Beth looked miserable. "So you're going to marry her?"

The thought still made him ill. But once the coming scandal of his breakup with Beth erupted across the country, he knew he'd have no choice. "Yes."

She bit her lip. "I saw her at the banquet, sitting beside the vizier. And I noticed..."

"What?"

She paused, then shook her head. "Forget it. It doesn't matter. Good night."

"Good night." Going to the door between their bedrooms, he paused. "Lock this door behind me."

"Why?" she joked weakly. "Are you afraid you won't be able to control yourself?"

"I still remember how it felt to make love to you, Beth. And you were right, what you told me in Paris." He looked at her. "Even though I'm a king, I'm also just a man."

She looked up at him, her luminous hazel eyes full of emotion, her sweet, full lips trembling. It took all of his willpower not to pull her into his arms. With a deep breath, she stepped back, out of his reach.

"I'll make your people hate me," she whispered.

With a stiff nod, he went into his own bedchamber, closing the door behind him. A moment later, he heard the bolt slide with a heavy *click*.

Now all he had to do, Omar thought grimly as he climbed into bed that night, was make himself hate her, too.

For the next few days, he tried to avoid Beth in the palace. He returned to his regular duties as King of Samarqara, while she was tutored in diplomacy, manners and the Samarqari dialect, for her future role as his consort.

But every time Omar saw her, whether from a distance or up close, he felt the same jolt. His feelings were all jumbled, anger and longing and desire. Desire most of all.

The days passed in a blur. As they waited to find out if she was pregnant, Beth upheld her promise, and seemed to try her best to do as he'd commanded. She watched Laila al-Abayyi's behavior, and did the opposite.

Laila was always perfectly elegant, dressed in black and white, either in chic versions of Samarqari traditional garb or designer outfits from Paris. So Beth used the allowance provided to her as future queen to buy cheap clothes from youthful shops in downtown Khazvin, in bright colors and styles, far too tight and with too much skin showing, wildly inappropriate for anywhere outside of Coachella, Glastonbury or Ibiza.

Laila was always formal, speaking only to her friends, her family's employees or wealthy people of her own class. So Beth chatted with everyone, palace servants, strangers in town, even the occasional straggling tourist. She played ball with children in the street.

Laila held lavish charity balls with an elite

international guest list, raising money for good causes. So Beth avoided fund-raising, instead spending her free time between lessons and palace duties, to help in Khazvin's homeless shelter. She used her own money to buy crafting materials and bring new computers to the widows' home and schools.

Beth did everything Omar had asked of her. Including avoiding him as much as he avoided her.

And every night, before he went to bed, he heard her carefully lock the bolt in the door adjoining their bedrooms.

Leaving him to many cold showers as he grimly waited out the time. How much longer would he be forced to endure this torture of having her live in his palace? How much longer, until they could know she wasn't pregnant—and they could part?

Finally, on court day, Omar's stamina ran out.

Each month, he held a session in his throne room when his subjects could come to the palace to speak with him directly about problems or issues. When, in the middle of court day, he was greeted by an entire family of seven, he looked at the parents in surprise. It was rare to have children brought to court. "You have business with me?"

"We have business with Dr. Farraday," the man said apologetically. "We wish to thank her."

"For saving our son," his wife said, smiling down at the dark-haired toddler in her arms. "Please, sire, will you permit us to see her? We have a gift for her."

"Of course," Omar said, even as his stomach churned. He nodded toward his guards. "Please ask my lady to come here."

When Beth appeared in the throne room, his mouth went dry.

She looked like sex appeal incarnate. Her light brown hair gleamed, tumbling down her shoulders. Her lips were scarlet red. Her hips swayed as she walked in on six-inch heels. Her curvaceous body was lathed in a tight, totally inappropriate tube dress in red.

But she greeted the family with quiet dignity, with her young maid following her. And though Omar ordered the queen's chair brought beside his, she didn't come to sit on the dais as was proper, as Laila certainly would have.

No. Beth walked directly to the mother, taking the woman's hands in her own. As her maid lifted up the child in her arms, they all spoke together, with the maid translating. They embraced each other, laughing. The parents handed Beth a rough, handmade plaster tile with a tiny hand-print in it, and the mother kissed both Beth's cheeks, as the father bowed his head and wept. At the end of it, they were all crying.

Not just the family. Not just Beth. Everyone in court looked teary-eyed, except for Khalid, who grimaced in irritation, and Hassan al-Abayyi, who tapped his foot impatiently. The two men were trying to hurry the end of the court day, so they could return to the small council chamber to begin discussions for a business deal.

Omar realized his eyes were wet, as well. He touched the corner of his eye in amazement, try-ing to remember the last time that had happened.

Watching Beth, he looked at the kindness and compassion and warmth radiating from her lovely face.

And then—he looked again at the tight red dress over her bombshell curves. He saw the outline of her nipples and realized *she wasn't even wearing underwear.*

Was she trying to make him lose his mind?

Beth hugged the family one last time, then turned and left the throne room. Without so much as looking at him.

Omar rose abruptly from his throne.

"Court day is over," he said.

"Sire," his vizier said in alarm, "you're not leaving? We still have the small council—"

"We have much to discuss," Hassan al-Abayyi said heavily. "Oil companies are waiting to hear if we'll auction the right to drill on our western border—"

"Later," Omar bit out. Hurrying down the steps from the dais, he left the throne room. People took one look at his face and cleared a path. Following Beth down the hall, he soon caught up with her with his longer stride.

Catching her elbow, he turned her to face him.

"You cannot," he ground out, "dress like that."

Still clutching the plaster tile of the child's handprint, Beth looked up at him in surprise. "I know I look hideous. I'm doing it to make everyone hate me, just as you wanted."

Having her sashay into his throne room looking like a sex goddess, when he was already tempted by the thought of her every single moment of the day, hadn't been exactly what he had in mind. "This is unbearable. Are you pregnant or not?"

She stared at him incredulously. "I still don't know."

"When will you?"

"Any day now."

He looked at her breasts, the outline of which were sharply revealed in the tight dress. Were they swollen? He couldn't tell. And just looking made him want to take her, right here in the palace hallway, right outside the throne room on court day. His heart pounded as he clenched his fists at his sides, resisting the temptation. "Go change your dress."

"Why? Isn't it working?"

It was working too well. That was the problem. Everything she was doing was making him want her more. In his bed. As his wife.

And in spite of her efforts, his people didn't seem to hate her. At least not the regular people of the city. He could still remember how they'd chanted her name that very first day. "Beth! Beth!" They loved her now, more than ever.

It was just his nobles who disliked her more. Samarqara's aristocrats watched her scandalous behavior and communicated their scorn to each other, not in open words, but with delicately raised eyebrows.

But that was nothing, compared to the way they'd react once they discovered that Beth Farraday wasn't a prodigy or world-famous scientist at all, but an ordinary shop girl.

If they discovered he'd been tricked, and had chosen such a woman over Laila al-Abayyi—

His hands tightened. He could imagine Hassan al-Abayyi going to war. The man had almost done it fifteen years ago, after the death of his oldest daughter. How would he react to another insult?

If only—

Looking down at Beth, Omar choked out, "I wish you were your sister."

She stiffened, and her lovely face looked stricken.

"I'm not Edith. I'll never be Edith."

Blinking fast, she fled up the steps to the tower.

With a low growl, he followed her to her bedchamber. When she tried to close the door in his face, he pushed it open.

Turning from him tearfully, Beth sat down on the sofa by the window. "Everyone wants Edith," she whispered. "She didn't even have to try, to make them love her. My parents. My grandmother. The world." She paused. "No matter how badly she treats people, she's loved. While I—"

She cut herself off, looking out the window. "Beth?"

When she didn't answer, Omar stood looking at her. His eyes slowly caressed down her pink cheeks, to her long throat and her luscious curves.

Forcing himself to turn away, he went to the small bar cabinet and poured them each a drink, in golden goblets encrusted with thick jewels.

Sitting beside her on the sofa, he quietly handed one to her.

She looked at it. "I shouldn't."

"Yours is club soda. In case…"

Beth lifted her gaze to his. "In case I'm pregnant with your baby."

His throat closed off as he pictured Beth, ripe with his child, her breasts swollen and full. His ring on her finger. Her eyes full of love.

No. He cut off the thought. He could not let himself want that. Or the disaster to his country that might ensue.

It was just an illusion, in any case. She'd never had any real feelings for him. None.

Leaning back against the sofa's cushions, he took a big gulp of his own vodka tonic.

"It would be a disaster if I'm pregnant, wouldn't it?" She gave him a sad smile. "You need a queen who is powerful and brilliant and successful. Otherwise, everyone will wonder why you didn't just choose a girl from home?"

He nodded. "Samarqara is prosperous and stable now, but it was not always so. In my grandfather's time, the country was nearly destroyed by war. And my own father was weak. He ignored my mother to chase his mistresses, and did whatever the nobles wanted."

"But you changed all that," Beth said slowly. For a moment, their eyes locked. He felt it again, the twist in his heart, that connection...

Taking another sip of the drink, he forced himself to say lightly, "Did you see Sia Lane in the news yesterday, claiming she only took part in the bride market as research for an upcoming role?"

Beth snorted, and her eyes danced. "She said that?"

"But when the reporter asked what movie it was for, she suddenly couldn't remember."

"Funny. Have you heard about Anna and Taraji?" she said, referring to the high-powered Sydney attorney and Silicon Valley executive.

"What?"

"They quit their jobs, which must have been what they really wanted all along. Anna's bought a vineyard in New Zealand. Taraji's opening a yoga studio in Marin."

For a moment, they smiled at each other. Then Beth's smile faded. "I don't blame Sia for trying to hide why she did the bride market. She doesn't want people to laugh at her." She looked down at her club soda. "Success is what matters in life. Wealth and power and fame. All things I wouldn't know what to do with, if I had them."

Trying not to look at the tight red dress, which at any moment was threatening to retreat and allow her breasts to fully spring free, Omar said, "There are all kinds of ways to be successful." He took a gulp of his drink. "Look at me. Who am I?"

"A king."

"A job I inherited my job from my father, who inherited it from his father. I told you that a king is like a servant. What glory is there in serving others?"

"Lots," Beth said. "Sacrificing oneself for others is the greatest glory of all. Not everyone realizes that."

Omar looked at her. "You do."

She snorted. "Me? I haven't done anything."

His eyebrows rose incredulously. "That's all you've done since you arrived in Samarqara. Helping others, volunteering, caring." He paused. "It was never about seeing Paris, was it? You pretended to be your sister in the bride market because she asked you. You did it for Edith."

"She's my sister. My parents died in a car crash when we were thirteen. Now our grandma's gone, she's all the family I've got left." Beth looked down at her hands in her lap. "I love her."

Sitting this close to her on the sofa was torture. As Omar breathed in her soft scent of honey and vanilla, he could remember how it felt to have her naked body against his own. Desire pounded through him. It took all of his self-control to look away.

He took another drink from his goblet.

"My experience of family was…very different. After my brother died, my father abandoned us for his mistresses and sports cars. My mother was heartbroken by my brother's death. She sent me off to boarding school in America so she wouldn't have to see my face, and be reminded of the son she'd lost." He turned away. "She rarely left her room. She couldn't bear to. She had to endure all my father's affairs without being allowed to divorce him."

"Oh, no." Beth looked stricken as she reached

for his hand. He looked down at her fingers, laced softly through his own.

"When I came to the throne, the nobles were stealing from the treasury, living in luxury as regular people starved. I vowed I would not be weak like my father. I'd rule like my grandfather. Without mercy."

Beth's eyes were huge in the warm afternoon light from the large windows of the queen's bedchamber.

He took a sip of his drink. "I was immediately under pressure to marry, and secure the throne with heirs." He gave a short smile. "I was twenty-one. In my infinite wisdom I thought, who better to be queen than the most beautiful girl in the land? And how better to tame the most powerful noble family, than with an alliance of marriage?"

Omar had never told this story to anyone. He stopped.

"What happened?"

His jaw tightened, and he looked away. "I proposed marriage. The girl accepted. But the morning before I was to marry Ferida al-Abayyi, she ran off to die in the desert rather than be my bride."

Beth gasped. For several moments, the only

sound was the cheerful birds singing in the garden beneath the tower.

Omar remembered how he'd waited in the palace that day, feeling at first amused by Ferida's lateness, then insulted. And then—then he'd gotten the news of what she'd done.

"How could she?" Beth whispered.

Staring down at his goblet, he said in a low voice, "She said in her suicide note it was because she loved another."

"Why didn't she just tell you that?"

Omar gave a low, harsh laugh. "It was the law then, that the king could choose any bride, and she was not allowed to refuse. Hassan al-Abayyi assured me his daughter wished to marry me. He insisted Ferida would quickly get over her shyness." He shook his head grimly. "I barely knew her. So I believed him. Because I wanted her."

He couldn't look Beth in the face. Setting his jaw, he said, "Her father wanted her to be queen. But she said in her note she'd already given her virginity to another man. She did not want to betray him. Or marry me under false pretenses, since by tradition the king's bride had to be a virgin."

"That's why you didn't care about virginity with me," she said slowly.

He gave a harsh laugh. "Ferida's death changed everything. When they found her body out in the desert…"

Shuddering, he couldn't go on.

"Who was the other man?" she asked suddenly.

Omar shook his head. "I never knew. Some stable boy, I expect. She was only eighteen." He tightened his hands. "I changed the laws so women could choose their own husbands. And for the last fifteen years, when my advisers begged me to marry, I refused."

"That's why you did the bride market?"

"I had to know my bride was willing. With no secrets."

Beth bowed her head guiltily. "Until I wrecked it by pretending I was Edith." She shook her head. "You never thought of just waiting to fall in love?"

"Love?" he said harshly. "I thought I was in love with Ferida. Love makes you blind." He thought of his father. "It makes you reckless and cruel."

"Not true love," Beth whispered.

He gave a hard laugh. "True love—what is that?"

She looked into his face. "When you care for someone so much, their happiness matters more than your own."

For a moment, Omar caught his breath. Then his shoulders tightened.

"I love my country. There's no room in my heart for anyone else."

Turning away, Beth gently set down her goblet. "It's funny. You don't even want to be loved. While I've dreamed of it my whole life, of being someone's most important person. And someday, after I leave here..." She lifted her chin. "Someday, I'll find someone who loves me. And we'll love each other forever."

Omar felt a sudden sharp pain in his throat. He rose unsteadily from the sofa.

"Then we must pray you're not pregnant, Beth," he said quietly. "So you can find your true happiness."

And he left her in the queen's bedroom without a backward glance, forcing his heart to stone.

CHAPTER NINE

THE NEXT MORNING Omar was in the small council chamber, beginning business negotiations with a multinational oil firm, when he got a panicked phone call from the only person he would have allowed to interrupt—Beth.

"I'm all right," were her first trembling words. All of Omar's senses went on alarm.

"What's happened?"

Her voice choked on a sob. Omar's heart lifted to his throat. Looking at the others in the room, he said harshly, "Leave. Now."

The powerful businessmen looked at him, then at each other. Reluctantly, they left. Only his vizier lingered, listening.

"What's happened?" Omar bit out, clawing his dark hair back as he paced in his Italian-cut suit.

"You know I was cutting the ribbon to help open the new clinic today." He heard the shock in her voice, the tears. "It was all good. Until some men in the crowd started yelling that I wasn't Dr. Edith Farraday, and I didn't deserve to be queen because I was really just a cheap tart who worked in a shop. I didn't know what to do. I froze. And then—then—" Her voice choked on a sob. "They started throwing things at me. Tomatoes at first...then rocks..."

Rage pulsed through Omar as he gripped the phone.

"I'm coming to get you," he bit out, heading for the door.

"No. I'm all right." Her voice broke. "Your bodyguard is driving me back to the palace. But..." She sounded pitiful as she whispered, "The back of your Rolls-Royce will have to be cleaned, from all the tomatoes dripping off me."

"I'll be waiting at the back door when you arrive," Omar said curtly, and hung up.

"What's happened, sire?" his vizier asked innocently.

"Somehow news got out about Beth."

"How?"

"I don't know," he said grimly. But whoever the men were, he wanted to kill them. With his bare hands. "Find out who leaked the story."

"Of course, sire," Khalid said. Bowing, he left.

Omar's whole body felt tight as he strode out of the small council chamber. His hands gripped into fists as he stalked down the halls. Servants took one look at his face and fled. He was still trembling with inchoate rage as he reached the private back entrance of the palace, beside the courtyard and twenty-car garage.

He waited for her car to arrive, pacing beneath the bright sunlight and softly waving palm trees of the paved courtyard. He hadn't waited for anyone since he became king. Others always waited for him. But he waited for her.

Omar couldn't stop thinking about the attack.

Beth had left that morning, not in a tight dress, but something equally inappropriate: oversize white denim overalls over a colorful striped T-shirt, with her light brown hair in a ponytail that made her look like an art student. She'd been excited to help open a medical clinic. She'd practiced her short speech in Samarqari over breakfast, repeating it over and over, anxious to make sure she pronounced everything right and didn't have a repeat of the disastrous donkey episode.

He could imagine Beth smiling and talking to everyone outside the new clinic, holding up a pair of ridiculously oversize scissors so she could ceremonially cut the big ribbon.

And strangers in the crowd had yelled insults

at her. Omar paced in fury, clawing back his hair. They'd thrown tomatoes at her. He stopped, snarling out a low curse. They'd thrown *rocks*.

He punched the stone wall of the palace, leaving his knuckles bloody and bruised.

"Sire!"

Omar turned in a rage. Khalid looked nervous, then squared his shoulders and came forward.

"I don't know how her true identity was discovered, but it's all over the news. The people are in uproar. They say if you marry her, you are a weakling and a fool."

"The people?" he ground out.

"The nobles," his vizier clarified. "But it seems the common people have turned against her, as well. How else to explain them throwing rocks?" His thin face sharpened. "What shall I tell the reporters, sire? May I announce that you intend to cast off the imposter, and marry the woman you should have chosen from the start—Laila al-Abayyi?"

Laila. Always Laila! The man was obsessed with her! Omar replied sharply, "I do not know yet if the queen is pregnant."

"You call that shop girl your queen?"

Omar stiffened. "You know she is, until the

day I divorce her," he said coldly. "Even if no one else knows that, you do."

Khalid bowed his head. "Of course." He looked up. "But if she's pregnant, you may still be rid of her. She is a proven liar. You do not have to claim the child as yours. You could—"

Omar turned on him with such ferocity, the other man shrunk back in fear. "You think I would lie and desert her and the child? You think so little of my honor?"

"My apologies. I was only trying to—"

"I know what you are trying to do," he said unsteadily.

The vizier paused. "You do?"

"You are trying to serve the throne, as always. And in recognition of your years of loyal service I will forget your insult." Then he saw the Rolls-Royce enter the courtyard and left Khalid without a word.

Before the car had even come to a full stop, Omar was opening the passenger door. He felt ill when he saw his beautiful wife, pale, her cheerful ponytail and white denim now bedraggled and covered in a mess of red splatters that, for one heart-stopping moment, looked like blood.

"I'm all right," Beth stammered. "Truly, Omar, I'm fine—"

He didn't believe her. Pulling her into his arms, he held her tight, until her trembling stopped.

"I'm getting tomatoes on your suit—"

"I don't care," he growled, holding her. Long moments later, he slowly pulled away. "The world has found out about the twin switch."

She tried to smile. "I guess that explains all the television cameras and vans lurking at the palace gate."

He gritted his teeth. "I swear I will find whoever leaked the story and…"

"It doesn't matter," Beth whispered. "I'm fine. Safe."

Safe, he thought bitterly.

"I'm sorry, Your Highness," the bodyguard blurted out, getting out of the front seat of the car. "One moment the crowd was cheering for her, and then—I never expected them to turn like that!"

Omar glared at him. "Send the doctor to the queen's bedchamber."

Nodding, the bodyguard fled.

Beth was still in his arms. Feeling her body against his caused a reaction that Omar couldn't control. For weeks, since the night of the engagement banquet, he hadn't touched her. Not so much as a kiss.

Every night, Beth had slept in the queen's suite, adjacent to his own. Safe on the other side of the bolted door.

Safe.

Omar took a deep breath. He'd never imagined his people could turn on her like that. They'd seemed to love her.

But he knew how violently loyalties could turn. He'd grown up hearing stories of how thousands of people had died, turning family against family, neighbor against neighbor, in the wanton destruction of Samarqara's civil war, barely sixty years before.

Now, Omar anxiously looked her over. "Did the rocks hit you?"

Beth shook her head. "They all missed by a mile." Looking down at her white denim overalls, now splattered with red, she said ruefully, "The tomatoes are another story."

What would have happened if the men had used weapons deadlier than tomatoes and rocks? He shuddered at the thought. "I'm taking you to your bedroom to rest. You'll be checked over by a doctor."

"I'm fine. I was scared more than anything—"

"You will see a doctor," he said harshly. When

she hesitated, he lifted her up against his chest and carried her, so she could not defy him.

His heart was still pounding. No longer with rage, but with fear.

What had he done, bringing Beth into his palace? Unlike Laila al-Abayyi, who'd been brought up in a powerful family and understood Samarqara's history, Beth naively believed the best of everyone. What place did she have in politics? What protection would she have, from those who might seek to hurt her, either with weapons, or with words?

None.

When they reached the queen's chambers, Omar gently set Beth down in the en suite marble bathroom. The late morning sunlight shone gold against the silver fixtures.

Turning on the shower to heat up the water, he looked down at her. Her eyes looked up at him, but she didn't say a word. When he put his hand on her shoulder, he felt she was suddenly shivering hard. As if the fear had finally, truly hit her.

Unbuckling the tops of her overalls, he let them drop to the floor. She did not resist as he lifted her arms to gently pull off her T-shirt, then her bra, then her panties. He wasn't thinking about her body. He was only thinking about how to comfort her. How to keep her safe.

He looked anxiously into her numb eyes. "Dr. Nazari should be here any moment."

"A male doctor," she said.

"No, the queen's doctor is always a woman. I'll let her in." He gently nudged her into the hot, steamy shower, and left without looking back. He didn't want to see his wife naked and pink with steam, standing in the glass shower. He could only endure so much.

The doctor arrived a few minutes later.

"Your betrothed is hurt?" Dr. Nazari asked.

"She was scared. So I want you to check. And—" he hesitated "—will you let me know if she's pregnant?"

The doctor looked at him, then slowly nodded. "If she wishes it."

"Thank you." He went into his own bedchamber to wait. He leaned his head back against the wall, exhaling.

If Beth was pregnant...

He wanted that desperately. And dreaded it.

He desired her as he'd never desired anyone. But he could not be selfish enough to keep her. Not when she might be in danger. Not when she dreamed of love. He had to let her go.

Unless she was pregnant.

If Beth was pregnant, he would be bound not just by law, but by honor, to keep her as his wife. And he would. Even if he had to defy his nobles, his people, the entire world.

Defy them, would he? A voice mocked. He hadn't even been able to protect Beth from his own people today!

And that would always be a risk. If she remained as his queen, she'd have to give up her country, her home, her freedom. And for what? She didn't care about wealth or power or fame. As she'd said, she wouldn't know what to do with them if she had them.

What Beth wanted was love. And Omar could not love her. He did not know how.

Dr. Nazari came out of the bedroom, her gray head bowed.

"Well?" he demanded anxiously.

"The Lady Beth is fine, Your Highness. Just a few cuts and bruises that I have bandaged. It could have been worse." Her dark eyes were kind. "She asks you go in and speak with her now."

With a deep breath, Omar went inside the queen's bedchamber.

The room was dark. The shades had been

drawn. He saw Beth's wan figure, now wearing loose pajamas, tucked into the bed. He sat down beside her. Her eyes were downcast.

"The doctor gave me good news. You're not hurt," he said, trying to keep his voice cheerful. "You'll soon make a full recovery."

"I have news for you, too," she whispered. She took a deep breath, then lifted her gaze to his. "I'm not pregnant."

Beth watched his handsome face turning to shock, then something else—grief? No, surely not.

"You—you are sure?" he said hoarsely.

Miserably, she nodded.

She'd been happy the last few weeks. She'd always wanted to help people, and as Samarqara's queen, she'd been able to do that. She'd been trying to learn the Samarqari language as quickly as she could. She'd loved talking to people from all walks of life—students, workers, elderly people. In spite of her awkwardness, they'd still made her feel welcome. Like she was home.

But it had all ended today.

Beth looked at Omar, sitting next to her on the bed. His handsome face was expressionless. Frozen. As if he didn't know how to react.

He was being kind, she thought. He had to be secretly relieved he could take Laila al-Abayyi as his queen.

She'd seen the good Omar did for the community. His country was prosperous, his people loved him. His gruff, ruthless exterior hid a kind heart, desperate to do right by his people, even if that meant sacrificing his own happiness.

Or hers. So as heartbreaking as it was, Beth knew she had to leave. Because Omar didn't love her, and he never would.

For too many years, she had thought she didn't deserve to be loved. She'd thought she was nothing special, that she was too ordinary.

But now…somehow, after being chosen as his bride, and living here in this place, acting as Omar's queen, she found that something had changed in her. She'd realized she deserved love as much as anybody.

And she would find it. Even if that meant leaving behind a man she could have loved, with all her body and heart and soul. She could easily have given him the rest of her life.

Even now, as she looked at him in the shadowy coolness of her bedroom, her heart cried out to stay.

But she couldn't.

"I'm sorry," she whispered.

"I'm glad." His expression was flat. "You are free now. Just as you wished."

Beth looked down at her tightly clasped hands over the blanket, willing herself not to cry. Her voice trembled as she said in a low voice, "So, how does the divorce thing work?"

She was proud of how casual her voice sounded. As if they were discussing something of little importance.

Emotion crossed his handsome face, emotion that was quickly veiled.

"It doesn't have to happen immediately. We can take our time." He took a deep breath. "I have no intention of just throwing you out—"

"Why not? More efficient that way." She kept her voice cheerful, to hide how her heart was breaking. "Better for the kingdom to end our secret marriage before the scandal goes any further."

Omar looked her straight in the eyes.

"Beth," he said in a low voice, "is there any reason why I shouldn't divorce you?"

"None." She looked away. What could she do, plead with him to choose her over his country? To make Beth his priority, instead of his duty to the throne? He didn't love her! "I'll leave today."

"At least let me call my lawyers, arrange a fair settlement for you. I don't want you to think—"

"I don't want your money." Her heart was aching. In another moment, she might break down into sobs. If this was the right thing for them both, why did she feel so awful?

"Beth, there's no reason to—"

"Please, Omar," she said softly. She couldn't meet his eyes. "Just let me go."

For a long moment, he said nothing. Then he covered her clasped hands with his own. For the first time, his skin was cold to the touch. As if the fire had gone out.

He repeated something to her three times. Then he said quietly, "Say the same words back to me."

She did, then waited, her whole body trembling with the effort it took not to collapse, to cling to him and beg him to let her stay and ask why, why, why, he couldn't love her.

Omar took a deep breath, and removed his hand.

"It's done," he said. "We're divorced."

She swallowed. "Just like that?"

"As it started, so it ended. The lawyers will have you sign a stack of papers before you leave, to make it all legal. Once it's filed with the courts this afternoon, it's official."

"Oh," she said dully. "Good."

Reaching out, he cupped her cheek and gave her a trembling smile. "You deserve a life of good things, Beth. Security. Freedom. And love. Love most of all. All the things I could never give you." He kissed her forehead. His voice broke as he whispered, "Goodbye, *habibi*."

And without another word, without another look, he walked out of Beth's life—forever.

Omar felt like he couldn't breathe as he watched Beth leave the palace an hour later, followed by servants carrying her suitcases and bags.

It was for the best, he told himself fiercely, standing in the window of the throne room. Beth was right. Ending it quickly, rather than drawing out the torture, would be a mercy to them both. Now they knew she wasn't pregnant, there was no reason to continue. Not when it was so destructive to his country's peace—and to Beth's.

Yet, as he'd spoken the words to divorce her, they'd tasted like ash in his mouth. And now, as he watched her leave, his body shook. He wanted to run after her, to grab her, to never let her go.

Is there any reason why I shouldn't divorce you?

None, she'd said. *Please, Omar. Just let me go.*

So he did not move. He could not keep Beth here, and watch as her spirit was broken, one tomato, one rock at a time. He could not force her to remain married forever to a man who did not know how to love her, even if he weren't already bound by endless duty to his country.

He could not trap another woman, watching the bright light inside her slowly fade, until, in her despair, she walked out into the desert to die.

His last blurry image of Beth Farraday as she climbed into the Rolls-Royce was from the same window of the throne room, where he'd first conceived of the bride market a few months before.

In spite of her objections, he'd arranged a settlement with his lawyers. An enormous sum would be wired to her bank account, waiting for her when she arrived in Houston. His private jet was already collecting Dr. Edith Farraday from his island in the Caribbean. She would be in Houston to greet her sister. He couldn't bear the thought of Beth being alone.

Someday, I'll find someone who loves me. And we'll love each other forever.

Beth was going to a better life. A better world. Where all her dreams could come true.

And as for him…

"The shop girl's gone, sire," his vizier said brightly behind him. "Shall we discuss your imminent engagement to Laila al-Abayyi?"

Omar didn't move. He'd never felt the chains of kingship more than right now. Or felt so alone.

He shut off all emotion. All feeling. All memory. It was the only way he knew to survive.

Numbly, Omar turned to him. "No engagement."

"But, Your Highness…" his vizier sputtered. "Surely you see that it's necessary. The country needs a firm hand!"

Omar looked down at his hands, which had so recently held Beth in his arms, but never would again. "No engagement," he repeated. "If Laila is willing to be queen, I want the wedding ceremony as soon as possible."

The vizier exclaimed in delight, "Sire!"

"Tomorrow," Omar said flatly. He looked back out the window. "I want this over and done with."

CHAPTER TEN

BETH WAS DOING the right thing.

The only thing.

She repeated that to herself, again and again, on the long flight to Houston. Trying to sleep, she stared numbly out the windows, looking down through the clouds as the private jet traveled over Europe, then the gray Atlantic. She'd done the right thing.

So why did her heart feel like it had been ripped out?

Omar deserved a better wife. A better queen. One who wouldn't be hated by his people and pummeled with rocks. She'd had to let him go.

But when Beth arrived in Houston at sunset, her shoulders were drooping and her heart felt sick. A limo was waiting for her on the tarmac of the private airport. As the driver loaded her luggage—just her rucksack, and a suitcase of cheap bohemian clothes from the funky shop in Khazvin—she wearily climbed into the back seat. Then she saw the person in the back seat waiting for her.

"Beth," Edith cried, holding out her arms.

Just seeing her sister's face, her eyes so concerned beneath her thick glasses, made tears finally flood Beth's eyes. Sobs choked her throat as she threw herself into Edith's arms.

Her sister murmured comforting words, stroking her back, saying, "I'm sorry, Beth, I'm so sorry. This is all my fault. I never should have convinced you to go."

But for her sister to blame herself was absurd. Beth pulled back, wiping her eyes. "It's not your fault. You're not the one who—" *The one who let yourself care for a man you knew you could not have.* She swallowed hard. "What are you doing here?"

"Your—King Omar sent his jet to collect me. He didn't want you to be alone."

As the limo's engine started, and the driver drove them away from the tarmac, the lump in Beth's throat thickened.

"Bastard," she whispered.

Edith looked confused. "He was just worried about you."

And that was what hurt most. Knowing that he cared. He actually cared.

But he'd still let her go. He didn't love her. Not like…

She stopped the thought cold. She couldn't even think it. She couldn't let it be true.

"How does it feel to be back?" Edith said.

Looking out at the Houston streets at twilight, Beth should have felt pleased to be back home. But all she could think about were the streets of Samarqara's capital city, the scent of salt and spice in the fragrant breezes off the Caspian Sea. She took a deep breath and changed the subject. "You look tan."

"I do, don't I?" She gave a very un-Edith-like grin. "Turns out I don't hate vacations as much as I thought. Especially—" Edith's grin widened "—after I met Michel."

"Michel?"

"He worked as a gardener on the king's estate. He's also a musician." Her eyes twinkled. "And very, very good with his hands."

Beth's lips parted. "Are you saying…"

"We spent lots of time together. We drank daiquiris and danced on the white sand beach by moonlight. It was incredible. So incredible that when I left, he quit his job to come live here with me. In fact…" Leaning forward in the back seat of the limo, looking right and left as if she thought the driver might be listening and judging her, she whispered, "He's waiting for me right now."

"Oh, Edith!"

"I've never been in love before. I always thought love was a waste of time. But now," she said dreamily, "I know when I come home from the lab at night, Michel will be there to play me songs on his guitar. And…" Her cheeks blushed as she gave a girlish giggle. "And all the rest."

"I'm so happy for you," Beth said, putting her hands over her twin sister's. And she was. How could she be anything but happy for Edith, now her sister had finally found love at last?

But the pain in Beth's own heart over what she'd lost—the man and country she'd left behind—was almost unbearable.

As the limo pulled down her street, Beth's lips parted when she saw crowds of television trucks outside her nondescript apartment building. "Has something happened?"

"You," Edith said. "You're famous."

"Me?" she said incredulously. Looking at the terrifying crowds of paparazzi and reporters, she leaned forward to the driver and begged, "Get us out of here." As he nodded and turned a sharp corner, she turned to her sister. "Why would I be famous in Houston?"

"The whole world wants the story of the shop girl who tricked a king into believing she was her twin, and into choosing her as his bride, even over Sia Lane." Edith smiled wryly. "If it makes you feel better, I can't go home, either. Michel and I checked into a hotel. The lab's getting pounded with calls. Television reporters. Newspapers. But it's not my story they want. It's yours."

"No," Beth said weakly.

"They're offering morning show interviews. Book deals. Even a reality show. Check your phone."

Beth turned it on. To her shock, she saw she had forty-one phone messages, and even more texts. She looked at her lackluster social media accounts, which she'd created years before to follow her favorite stars and connect with friends. Her eyes went wide.

"I have eight million followers." She was suddenly shaking. "What's going on?"

"You're famous, Beth. Everyone wants to know you. You're special."

"But how can I work at the thrift shop, with people following me?"

Edith paused. "I don't think you need to worry about that."

Beth snorted. "The forty dollars in my checking account says otherwise. And I'm not selling Omar's story to the press. Not for any price!"

Her sister peered at her as if she was a specimen under a microscope. Then she gave a satisfied nod. "Ah."

"What do you mean by that?" Beth said, disgruntled.

"When your king called me…"

"Omar called you directly?"

"Yes." Edith smiled. "He made it clear that you'll never need to work again. *Tell her to follow her heart. Make her do it*, he told me. He also asked me for the numbers of your bank account." She shrugged. "Easy enough to find. You've used the same password since high school, Bethie. TrueLove1."

"Edith!" she cried.

"Check your bank account."

Glowering, Beth looked up her bank details on her phone. Since all her bills were on autopay, she expected to see she had forty-one dollars left. She'd counted on getting back to work at the shop immediately. She'd been a little worried about next month's rent.

No longer. Her eyes boggled.

Beth had fifty million dollars.

Just sitting there. In her checking account. She had to keep counting the zeroes to be sure she wasn't counting them wrong.

"Why would he do this?" she whispered, feeling dizzy.

Her sister looked at her. "Can't you think of a reason?"

Beth felt topsy-turvy inside. "I'll give the money to you—"

"No." Edith's voice was firm. "He was very clear to me on this point. This money is for you and you alone. But don't worry—" She grinned suddenly, and said in a cheerful voice, "My research has now been completely and utterly funded for the next ten years."

"That's wonderful," Beth said slowly.

But she suddenly faced a life she couldn't recognize. She thought of all the cameras and people outside her dilapidated studio apartment and shivered.

She'd always wanted to be special. But this was too much. And right as she was sitting there in shock, holding her phone, she got a text.

It was from Wyatt, the boyfriend who'd broken up with her because she "wasn't special."

His new message said:

I've made a horrible mistake. Meet for coffee?

"Wyatt wants to give our relationship another chance," she said in a strangled voice.

"Of course he does, Beth." Her sister's voice was soft. "Do you know, I've always been a little envious of you?"

Beth looked up in shock. "You—envious of *me*?"

"I've often wished I could live like you do. With such joy in every day. You bring happiness to so many. I don't think you even realize it."

She stared at Edith. All this time she'd been envying Edith, and her sister envied *her*?

Beth suddenly grinned. "Sure," she said. "And all you do is cure cancer."

"There is that," Edith agreed, returning her smile. Then she sighed. "The truth is, I don't know if I'll ever have that breakthrough. It's always just over the horizon. I might be wasting my life for nothing. And then I look at you. You don't waste a day. You don't waste a moment. Until I met Michel, I never knew how good it was."

"Sex?"

"Love." Her sister looked at her though her thick glasses. "You love him, don't you? This king of yours?"

Love him?

Beth's heart lifted to her throat.

She couldn't love him. He was a billionaire king. She was just a shop girl from West Texas.

She admired him, of course. She desired him. Okay, so obviously she was wildly infatuated, but who wouldn't be?

They were also friends. She cared for him. Respected him. She trusted him. He was the first person she thought of every morning, the last before she fell asleep. All she wanted on earth was his happiness. All she wanted was—him.

Because she loved him.

Beth sucked in her breath, covering her mouth with her hands as it hit her, the thing she'd tried so hard not to know. The thing she'd tried so hard to hide, even from herself.

"What is it?" Edith said gently.

Eyes wide, Beth turned to her in the back of the limo. She choked out, "I love him."

"I knew it," her sister said, then frowned. "So why did you leave?"

Beth's lips parted. "Because…because he didn't want me."

"That's empirically not true. All the evidence clearly shows that he cares for you desperately."

She thought of the emotion in Omar's dark eyes as he'd said in a low voice, *Is there any reason why I shouldn't divorce you?*

Beth swallowed hard. "He's King of Samarqara. He'll always put his people first. And the people don't want me."

"From the stories on the news, that's not true. They're heartbroken you're gone."

"They threw rocks at me. Yelled I wasn't worthy to be queen."

"All of them?"

"Some men in a crowd."

"And you agreed with those idiots, rather than trying to prove them wrong?"

"They weren't wrong!" Beth protested. "I'm not you."

"No doubt," her sister agreed. "You'd be a better queen than I'd ever be. I'm sure you weren't cooped up in a lab, but out in the community, taking care of people. Like you always do." When Beth bit her lip sheepishly, Edith gave a sharp nod. "Right. If you love him, you have to fight."

Fight for him? For a moment, hope lifted wildly inside Beth. Then it came crashing down.

"But Omar doesn't love me. He said so. He only loves his people."

"But does he know how you feel? Did you tell him?"

Beth looked out at Houston's passing city lights as twilight deepened. "No," she whispered.

"So do it."

"I can't."

"Why?"

"What if I try, and fail?"

Edith whirled on her, her eyes ablaze. "Do you have any idea how many times I've failed? More than I can count. Failure is part of success. You have to commit. That's the magic. The only magic. You give everything. And when you have nothing left to give, you give some more."

Staring at her twin sister, Beth felt her breath *whoosh* out of her lungs.

"You've never let yourself commit to anything, Beth. Not since we were kids." Edith shook her head. "You didn't want to risk becoming like me, closed off to everything beyond the lab. I was a cautionary tale."

Beth stared at her sister.

"No," she whispered. "You were my shining example. You found what you loved, what you were born to do. And you threw yourself into it, heart and soul. I never committed to anything because I was waiting to fall in love. I never found that." Her eyes went wide as she sucked in her breath. "Until now."

She'd always thought of herself as ordinary, a girl who wasn't particularly good at anything. A mediocre student who couldn't finish a degree or find a real career or attract a decent boyfriend. She'd blamed herself, for not trying hard enough. For not being good enough.

But she hadn't failed. In her heart, she'd never wanted those careers or those degrees or those men.

Then, in Samarqara, when she'd finally found everything she'd ever dreamed of, a man she loved, a job she loved, a place she loved, she'd gotten so used to giving up, she didn't even know how to put up a fight anymore.

Beth lifted her chin, her hands clenching.

Well, that would all change now.

Even if she tried and failed, even if she threw herself at Omar's feet and he scorned her, he deserved to at least know that she loved him. And she deserved to tell him.

All this time Beth had thought she wasn't worthy to be his wife. But she was. Because no one loved him more.

"Take me back to the airport," she told the driver, who nodded and turned the wheel.

"You're going back?" Edith said happily.

"I'm going to tell him. You're right." She hugged her sister. "I'm going to take the first flight back to Samarqara."

Her phone rang. Thinking it was another reporter, she was going to ignore it. Then she saw the Samarqara country code.

Beth snatched up the phone. But it wasn't Omar. It was someone even more startling.

"My lady, it's Rayah," the young maid said desperately. "You must come back to Samarqara. Please!"

"I am—but why? And why are you whispering?"

"I'm calling you from a closet in the tower so no one can hear. It's not even dawn but the king's wedding preparations have already started."

Beth's heart fell. "He's marrying Laila already?"

"I overheard the vizier talking to her in the garden. They are planning to poison the king's goblet in the wedding toast!"

"What?" Sitting up straight in the back seat of the limo, Beth gripped the phone. Her eyes went wide as she heard the details. Blood drained from her body. "You must warn the king!"

"I tried, my lady. But the king's beyond all reason. He's refusing to see anyone."

"Tell the people—have them storm the palace!"

"It would only give the vizier a better excuse for a coup. He's already blocking all access to the king. You're the only one who can get past his guards now."

"When will they do it?" Beth cried.

"The wedding will be private, tonight at midnight in the palace garden. As soon as they're wed, they'll kill him and seize the throne."

"I'm on my way," Beth cried. Hanging up, she tried to call Omar, but it went directly to voice mail. She tried again, but to no avail.

"What's happened?" Edith demanded.

"Omar's in danger." Leaning forward to the driver, she begged him, "Hurry, please hurry!"

Checking her phone, she saw the next commercial flight to Samarqara didn't leave for hours, and had a layover in Europe. She clawed back her hair.

Oh, why had she ever left him? All the thoughts of the future they could have had, if only she'd been brave enough to fight for it, flew through her mind.

"I'll never make it in time!"

"Oh, yes, you will." Edith's eyes, identical to her own, shone with faith. "Now that you know you love him, nothing can stop you."

As the limo drove past the private airport where she'd arrived, Beth had a sudden idea. "Turn here!"

"Not the international airport, miss?"

"No! Here!"

She nearly cried when she saw Omar's huge private jet still on the tarmac. They'd obviously already refueled and were getting ready to leave when she raced up the steps to the open door, Edith behind her.

"You must take me back to Samarqara," Beth panted.

The pilots and flight attendants looked at each other, then at Edith behind her.

"I'm sorry, Dr.—er—Miss Farraday," one said awkwardly. "The vizier said—"

"I don't care what the vizier said. The king's in danger." When they didn't move, she said desperately, "I will pay you fifty million dollars to take me back!"

When they still didn't move, Beth marched

into the cabin of the jet and sat down. Nervously, Edith followed her lead.

Looking at the pilots and flight attendants, she ordered, "You will start the engine. Now!"

The pilots and flight attendants looked at each other, then with a bow, rushed to obey.

"I didn't know you could do that," Edith whispered in her ear as the engine warmed up.

"I didn't, either," Beth muttered. As the jet started down the runway, she looked out the window at the wing, wishing she could go out and push it to make them go faster. Because as fast as they were going, she might not be in time to save the man she loved.

Omar paced in the moonlit palace garden where, in just a few moments, he'd be wed in a small private ceremony. There had been no time to arrange a grand public affair, but this was even smaller than he'd imagined. The only guests would be Laila and himself, with the vizier and Laila's father as witnesses. There would be no reception. A small table had been set up for the traditional wedding toast, right there in the garden, with the garden's verdant flowers and a few torches to decorate the ceremony.

"We'll have a more formal public coronation

later," his vizier had said brightly. "But for now, after all the…publicity of your last bride—" He'd paused and then continued, "it's best to keep this private."

Khalid had seemed almost *too* happy about it. But he had wanted Omar to marry Laila al-Abayyi from the beginning.

Omar looked down at his formal robes, with a silver dagger at his belt, the mark of the bridegroom. Marrying Laila was a necessary sacrifice. He'd spoken with her that afternoon, and she'd confirmed she was still willing to marry him. He had to marry someone sometime. It might as well be her, now.

So why did it feel so wrong—wrong in every way?

Why did he feel like his vizier was forcing him to wed a woman he didn't even like, let alone desire?

No. That wasn't fair. It wasn't Khalid's fault. Omar was the one who'd demanded the bride market. He was the one who'd chosen Beth, then secretly married and seduced her. And he was the one who'd demanded the immediate ceremony with Laila tonight. He'd wanted to put some barrier between himself and the past.

Between himself and Beth.

She was gone now. Gone to be happy in Houston, with her sister. Beth was rich now, famous. Special to all the world. But she'd always be more than special to him.

Taking a deep breath, Omar looked at his watch, an heirloom from his great-grandfather's day. Just a few minutes until midnight.

He paced through the dark palace garden. Moonlight frosted the edges of the palm trees sighing above like shadows. He heard the burble of the nearby fountain and, against his will, remembered that other garden in Paris, when Beth had first exploded into his life like a comet.

His heart twisted. He'd let her go so she could find happiness. So she'd find true love. At least he could be proud of that.

But he had to think of his nation. A low, ugly undercurrent of anger had spread across the city at the news of Beth's departure. Apparently, many of the common people still loved her. Whoever had thrown rocks at her in the crowd had disappeared without a trace. Many people said they didn't care if Beth was a scientist or a shop girl. They demanded she return as queen.

"The people are fickle, sire," his vizier had said with a shrug. "Who knows what they'll demand next? But I'll put the palace on lockdown, just in case." His thin lips had curved as he'd said, "They'll soon learn who's in charge."

Who *was* in charge? Omar wondered as he paced the moonlit garden. He stopped. Surely not he. If he were in charge, he would have Beth in his arms right now. He would be kissing her, feeling her soft body against his own. She would be his wife, now and forever.

But he'd divorced her. Set her free. He didn't want her to be trapped in this palace. He didn't want her to be unhappy.

He loved her.

He heard the echo of his own voice from what felt like long ago. *True love—what is that?*

When you care for someone so much, she'd replied, *their happiness matters more than your own.*

Omar looked up with an intake of breath.

He loved her.

"Sire." His vizier entered the dark garden. "Your bride is on her way. It's time."

"I can't," Omar breathed.

Khalid frowned. "What?"

"I love her," he whispered.

"You love your bride? Excellent. In a moment, you'll speak your vows, then we'll toast the future…"

"Not Laila," Omar said harshly. "Beth." His voice softened as his heart soared. Why had he never seen it before? "I love Beth." He started to turn. "I must go to her—"

"You cannot be so selfish, Omar."

His vizier had never spoken to him so harshly. He looked back in astonishment. "Selfish?"

"Would you see this country fall back into civil war? To see our city again become a ruin? To see innocents suffer—merely because you want that shop girl back in your bed?"

Omar took a deep breath. "No. But—"

"You cannot insult Laila like this. Not after what you did to Ferida."

"What I…did to her?"

"Forcing her to marry you against her will," Khalid said coldly. "And now you will scorn and humiliate her half sister? Hassan al-Abayyi will not forgive again. You must know this." His vizier came closer, his eyes gleaming in the moonlight. "You cannot turn back now. You must act like a king."

Like a king, Omar thought dimly.

Just then, Laila walked into the garden, on the arm of her proud father. She looked beautiful and regal in her traditional Samarqari gown and bridal headdress. Omar thought of his kingdom and tried to steel himself for this last, most important sacrifice.

But he could not do it.

His heart was Beth's. He could not pretend otherwise and marry another. For that would be the ultimate lie, the betrayal of his very core. And what kind of king, what kind of ruler could he be, without a heart? Without a soul?

For the first time, he understood why Ferida had fled to the desert rather than wed him against her will. For he was willing to do that now.

For Beth, Omar would set the whole world on fire.

"I'm sorry." He looked between Laila and her father. "I have great respect for your family. But this marriage cannot go on."

The other three looked at each other in astonishment.

Hassan al-Abayyi's face turned red beneath the torchlight as he sputtered, "If you even *think* you can..."

The vizier cut him off with a smooth gesture. Lifting his face into a bland smile, he said benignly, "If the king cannot wed today, then he cannot, and there is no more to be said."

Omar looked at his distant cousin with gratitude. "Thank you, Khalid."

Turning to the nearby table, the vizier poured wine into four golden goblets. "We will toast to the future, and the friendship that will always exist between the throne and the al-Abayyi family." He held out one of the goblets to Omar. "Surely you mean no insult to their honor."

"None," Omar said, relieved they were taking it so well. He took the goblet. Glancing at each other, the others took their goblets from the table.

The vizier held up his wine. "To the future of the kingdom."

"To the future," Omar said. He didn't notice the three pairs of eyes watching him avidly. As he lifted the goblet to his mouth, his mind was already on Beth. He could hardly wait to tell her he loved her. As soon as he'd finished this toast, he'd fly to Houston and offer his heart at her feet—

Smiling to himself, he pressed the goblet to his lips, and tilted his head back to drink.

"No!" a woman screamed, and the goblet was knocked out of his hand.

To his shock, Beth stood before him, her eyes wide with what seemed like panic. She wasn't in

Houston as he'd pictured her, but right in front of him now. And he'd never seen anything more beautiful, more wonderful, in his whole life.

"Did you drink anything?" she begged. "Did you?"

Suddenly, there were guards all around them in the garden. The vizier looked at them wildly, pointing at Beth. "Seize this woman!"

But the guards didn't move. They were looking at Beth for their orders, Omar realized.

"What are you doing here?" he breathed.

"Your drink was poisoned." Beth pointed at Khalid, Laila and Hassan al-Abayyi. "They were going to murder you and take the throne."

"She's lying!" Khalid cried.

"Murder me?" Omar said slowly, as the words penetrated the fog of his joy. He looked at Hassan, whose face was red with rage.

"Don't," Khalid said warningly.

But the older man was past all advice. He turned on Omar in fury. "You're ruining this country. All your talk of prosperity and equality for the common people. They need to be ruled with an iron hand, as in your grandfather's time!" He pointed at his daughter and the vizier. "Laila and Khalid know this. They should rule, not you!"

Omar staggered back in shock. He looked at Laila.

"I didn't know for sure they were planning to kill you," she said weakly. "I just wanted to be queen."

Looking at the vizier, Omar choked out, "And you. We've been friends since we were boys."

Khalid looked back at him with undisguised hatred. "We were. Until the day you murdered Ferida."

Omar gasped. "You were the man she loved?"

"And you took her from me," Khalid said tightly. "Just by right of being king. Ever since, I've dreamed of my revenge. I wanted your crown. When you married that shop girl, I thought I'd have to kill you on your honeymoon and seize the throne. Now I'll have to be satisfied," he said in a low growl, "with killing your woman!"

Khalid sprang murderously toward Beth, a knife in his hand.

Ripping his own ceremonial dagger from his belt, Omar blocked his blade at the last moment. They struggled, then Omar threw him forcibly to the ground.

"Take them," he said to the captain of the guard, who nodded grimly. A short scuffle ended with the three plotters being dragged away screaming, all of them blaming each other.

"What will happen to them?" Beth said brokenly, watching as they were taken forcibly out of the royal garden.

"I don't know or care." Pulling her into his arms, Omar fervently kissed her forehead, her cheeks. Emotion ripped through him, as he felt how he'd nearly lost her. Just remembering how Khalid's knife had gleamed wickedly in the light made his body shake. Holding her tight, he whispered, "You came back to me."

"Rayah called me in Houston. She'd heard the vizier plotting but no one could reach you. I couldn't let them hurt you. I…" As she looked up at him, her voice choked, and she turned away.

He gripped her hand, not releasing her. "What?"

"I came to tell you something, but…" Beth lifted her gaze miserably to his. "I can't. You married her. She's your wife."

Omar slowly shook his head. "I couldn't marry her." Lifting her limp hand, he pressed it against his heart and said tenderly, "How could I, when I want only you?"

Her eyes grew wide. "But you were in the middle of the wedding toast—"

"I canceled the ceremony at the last moment. So Khalid suggested a toast to the future." He scowled. "Now I see it was a future where he and Laila would rule."

Beth looked dazed. "How did they intend to claim the throne?"

"He probably intended to announce the wedding and my unexpected, sudden death. Then he'd claim the throne as the only male heir left, consolidating power by marrying the new queen."

"How dare he?" she cried furiously.

"But they failed." Omar looked down at her with tears in his eyes. "Because of you."

Beth was dressed in the same jeans and T-shirt she'd left the palace in, a day and a half before. Her eyes were tired, her glorious light brown hair frosted silver by moonlight. He'd never seen anyone who looked so beautiful, or more like a queen. He took a shuddering breath.

"You burst into my life like a flame," he whispered. He cupped her cheek, looking at her luminous face in the flickering torchlight of the garden. "Like the sun."

He felt her tremble beneath his touch, saw her lips part and her breasts rise and fall quickly beneath the T-shirt. "Omar...there's something I have to tell you."

"There's something I have to tell you, too. Something I should have said long ago." He met her gaze. "It doesn't matter what your name is, Beth. In my heart, from the moment I saw you in Paris, I knew you were the one."

"You did?" she said faintly.

"You have won the hearts of my people." He straightened. "I offer you the whole city. The love of an entire nation."

"It's not the nation's love I need," she said in a low voice.

The meaning of her words exploded in his heart, and he fell to his knees before her.

"I offer you my love, as well." Taking her hands in his own, he looked up at her. "You are strong and honest and fierce. You are the woman I want. I love you, Beth. And I will strive every day to..."

He looked away.

"To what?" she breathed.

He looked up at her. His eyes were blurry with tears as he spoke the truth from his heart. "To be worthy of you. If you'll just give me a chance to earn your love..."

"Earn my love? You can't." His heart fell to

the ground, until she choked out, "It's already yours. I was coming back to you even before Rayah called. To tell you I love you."

A thrill went through his heart.

"You love me?" he whispered, searching her gaze.

Wordlessly, she nodded, smiling though her tears.

Omar didn't remember how he got to his feet. Afterwards, he remembered only the sensation of flying. When he pulled her into his arms and kissed her, he soared.

For the first time in his life, he truly felt like a king.

A year later, spring had finally arrived in Samarqara. Spring, and Beth's sister.

"They're beautiful," Edith breathed, looking down at one-month-old Tariq in Beth's arms.

"The most beautiful babies in the world," Omar agreed, with his typical modesty where his newborn twins were concerned. He looked down at the baby snuggled in his own arms, Nyah, who was just two minutes younger than her brother.

"Twins," Edith said wryly, shaking her head. "I still can't believe it."

Sitting in a shady spot in the palace garden, beside the newly blooming flowers beneath the palm trees, Beth looked up at her sister fondly. "Think of all the fun they'll have."

"The fun's already begun," Omar said with a grin, stretching his arm along the top of the bench behind his wife. "I thought the kingdom went crazy at Beth's coronation…"

"We remember," Edith said, smiling at her new fiancé, Michel.

"But when the babies were born…" Shaking his head, Omar gave a low chuckle. "A great end for the newspapers. Let's just say the tourist board is very happy."

"Tourist board?" Michel looked confused.

"Tourism is up a thousand percent," Beth told him succinctly. *Take that, Sia Lane*, she thought.

"Oh." The young man looked bewildered, but nodded. "That's good."

Based on her sister's description, Beth had expected Michel Dupree to be a wild, sexy musician, but when Edith had brought him to their wedding and Beth's coronation ten months earlier, she'd discovered a quiet young Haitian, kind and talented, who now worked as a music teacher by day and a musician at night, but whose full-time job was really taking care of Edith.

"He cooks for me. Every night," Edith had confided. She'd giggled. "Then he *cooks*, if you get what I'm saying."

Now, looking at the two of them in the palace garden, Beth saw Michel put his arm around Edith tenderly. Her sister had truly found happiness in love, as well as work, where, as she always liked to say, she was closer to a breakthrough every day.

There were breakthroughs of all kinds, Beth thought. When she'd been brave enough to tell Omar she loved him, everything else had fallen into place. Now, she had a life more wonderful than she'd ever dared dream.

Their royal wedding had been magnificent. Nothing quiet or restrained about it. It had been a full royal affair, with twelve hundred guests from around the world, held in the grand palace. Beth had arrived via horse-drawn carriage, her traditional gown covered with jewels. She'd left on Omar's arm, the crowned Queen of Samarqara.

She still had the actual crown, kept mostly in the vault for special occasions. It was so heavy with diamonds, it hurt her head to wear it for too long. So she mostly didn't.

Beth. A queen. She still couldn't believe it.

The entire kingdom had come out to cheer that day. Even the nobles had cheered, if only to prove they hadn't been part of the attempted coup. Later, three men had shamefacedly come forward and confessed they were the ones who'd been hired by the vizier to throw rocks at Beth.

"We only did it because he threatened our families. We made sure none of the rocks came close to hitting you. Please, we throw ourselves on your mercy, our queen!"

After Beth's pleading, Omar had let the men go with nothing but community service as punishment. But Khalid and Hassan al-Abayyi weren't so lucky. They'd been sentenced to prison for life, their money and estates confiscated. Laila, as an accessory instead of active participant, had received exile. But bereft of her family's fortune, she screamed and begged to be sent to prison, too. "For what's the point of living if I can't live in a palace?"

It was ironic. Omar hadn't wanted the throne. He'd taken it as a duty he was honor-bound to endure. Beth had never dreamed of living in a palace, either. Why would she? The demands of royalty had nearly torn them apart.

But the two of them, by loving each other, had

somehow managed to make this gilded cage of a palace into the homey cottage of Beth's dreams.

It was love that changed everything, she thought in wonder. Love could take even a palace and make it a home.

Love, and family.

They'd conceived their twins on their wedding night, in the same bed they slept in now. "I saved this bed only for you," Omar had whispered in her ears. "To make love only to my wife. My queen."

She blushed, remembering. He wanted a large family. He was threatening to get her pregnant a *lot*. Six, perhaps seven more times. And given the way he kissed her, the way he made her body come so alive, she didn't think she'd be able to refuse. Fortunately, a large family sounded just fine to her.

As international media broadcast images of the popular King and Queen of Samarqara, so obviously in love, and now with newborn twins, there was some talk that bride markets—and groom markets—might be the best way to find true love after all. Reading an American newspaper the other day in their bedroom, sitting together near the fire as their babies slept, Beth burst into a laugh. "This article says you're a genius!"

"Of course I am," Omar had told her loftily. "I know everything. That is why you must always obey me, wife."

Then he'd said *ooph* as she smacked him playfully with a pillow.

Now, Beth looked at her husband in the dappled sunlight of the palace garden. As the two of them cuddled together on the shady bench, and her sister and almost-brother-in-law drank mint tea and exclaimed over their tiny sleeping babies, Beth still couldn't understand how she'd been so lucky. What had she ever done to deserve a life like this?

Then she knew.

One thing had changed her life. When she'd found it, nothing could stop her. Not danger, not fear, not doubt. When she'd found it, she'd found her strength. Found herself.

Just one thing: love.

* * * * *

LET'S TALK

Romance

For exclusive extracts, competitions and special offers, find us online:

- **f** facebook.com/millsandboon
- **⊙** @millsandboonuk
- **🐦** @millsandboon

Or get in touch on 0844 844 1351*

For all the latest titles coming soon,
visit millsandboon.co.uk/nextmonth

*Calls cost 7p per minute plus your phone company's price per
minute access charge